The Lady Upstairs

The Lady Upstairs

Eleanor Trevithick

Rev. date: 06/12/2015

To order additional copies of this book, contact:
Xlibris
1-888-795-4274
www.Xlibris.com
Orders@Xlibris.com
705336

CHAPTER 1

Millie Houston was reading to her four-year-old granddaughter when they heard the sound of tires on the gravel driveway. "Mommy's here, Mommy's here," called Betsy, as she jumped down from her grandmother's lap.

"How do you know it's your mother?"

"I heard the scrooch on the baby stones. It's her car."

Kendra came breezing into her mother's house. She was excited and happy as she gathered up Betsy with a hug, and turning to her laughing mother asked, "What's so funny, Mom?"

"Later, later," as she tried to stop laughing. "Just learned some new words," then she got serious. "What were you so excited about when you came in?"

"Mom, my problem is solved. Yes, I am excited!," she said, as she whirled with Betsy in her arms, then sat down in a kitchen chair. "I'm renting out that bedroom and bath at the top of the stairs. That will give me enough extra income to send Betsy to pre-school while I'm at work."

"School...school? I'm going to school?" asked Betsy.

"Shh, yes dear," her mother said, hugging her closer.

"Oh, Honey," Millie said quickly, "I didn't know there was any problem to solve. I like having Betsy with me, and I can surely do that little bit."

Her daughter replied excitedly, "You'll still have plenty of time with Betsy that will help a lot--but only on the days you feel like it. This will work out great, you'll see. Mrs. Druise at 'Toddler Town' said I could bring Betsy in on the days you couldn't manage or were busy. She has three "On Call" helpers which will work for everyone." Then to Betsy, "You really will love it. There will be others your age to play with and you'll like that, won't you?"

Betsy asked, "Will I learn to read at school?"

"You will when you get older. I'm not sure you will start reading at this school, but I promise whatever they do it will be fun."

"If I took care of her full time I could teach her to read," said her mother.

Kendra laughed, and said, "Mom, you're not fighting fair."

Her mother laughed too and replied, "Well on the days she's with me that's what we will do." Betsy hopped down from her mother's lap and ran to check out her books kept at her grandmother's house.

Kendra said, "you need days off to do other things, like your Bid-Whist days with your friends, lunches or a matinee, and other days to just rest and do quiet things and of course, it will be great for Betsy."

"If only Benny Schyler was still available," said her mother.

"Yes he was good with Betsy, but he's working full time now. This will work even better as Betsy will be getting used to being with other children."

Millie sighed in resignation then said thoughtfully, "Yes, of course she should get used to being with other children. I have never met Mrs. Druise, but I have heard good things about 'Toddler Town' and if that's what you want----Who is she? -- the tenant I mean. Someone you know?"

"No. One of our substitute teachers mentioned this writer who needed a small apartment or room. She had been recommended by her neighbor of many years. Be happy for me, Mom. This is what I want. You'll still have Betsy when you feel like it, and I'll be doing it on my own."

"You were on your own for a long time before you were married and got along just fine," her mother reminded her.

"But I didn't have Betsy depending on me then. Everything was different. It was fun being on my own and I really hadn't thought much about getting married. I was pretty satisfied with my life until I met Therm. Then it was different and I wanted a life with him. It's hard getting along without him and now I have Betsy and full responsibility for her as well as being older than most mothers with a four-year-old child. With that extra income from the tenant I'm sure

I can handle it," and she sat up straighter and squared her shoulders. Then she added, "Even if I didn't have this precious child I would always be thankful that I had Therm's love and company for those few years."

Her mother sighed and said, "Then I wish you luck and hope it all works out--and when I can help, I want to."

Betsy came back into the room and cuddled up to her mother. "Do you know what?"

"No. What?"

"Grammy let me set the table, but I walked when I took the dishes to the table."

"Oh," her mother asked with a grin, "you took the bus other days?"

"Nooo, Mommy," she giggled, "I used to run, but Grammy said I should walk when I'm carrying dishes."

"Well I think that makes good sense, don't you?" asked her mother, laughing.

"Yeah, I guess. And we had half a Condo for lunch."

Her grandmother said, "That was a Klondike Bar. A Condo is the place where Mrs. Chandler lives. Remember?" Then she turned to Kendra and said, "We had salmon and peas on mashed potatoes first."

"I don't think you ever served it that way when I was home. It was always salmon wiggle on biscuits or toast points."

"I told Grammy it was hard to eat those things," said Betsy, "so she said I could have it on mashed potatoes, and it was good."

Kendra said thoughtfully, "I can see how much you help Betsy and I know it will be a good mix with you helping some days and Betsy getting to mingle with children on other days. I feel really good about this arrangement."

"Then I'm happy about it too," her mother added.

After her daughter and granddaughter had left, Millie sat in her recliner thinking of her beautiful daughter with her bouncy, dark hair and lovely figure. Who would have dreamed that her and Therm's lives together would have been so short. He had died two years before while doing what he loved--racing cars. Millie had been afraid her only child was so wrapped up in her career that she would never want to get married, but when she met Thurm everything changed. When Betsy was born, Millie's dreams had come true. She had her grandchild at last. It no longer mattered that some of her closest friends already had great grandchildren.

Millie realized how rough a time it had been for Kendra when Therm died, especially so soon after losing her own dad then trying to cope with little Betsy alone. Millie then started wondering about the stranger coming to live in the cottage with Kendra and Betsy.

CHAPTER 2

One morning Kendra had stopped in to see her mother after dropping Betsy off at Toddler Town. As they were having coffee at the kitchen table Millie asked, "Is Betsy still having fun at school?"

"Mom, she absolutely loves it. Mrs. Druise says she asks occasionally when they are going to learn to read. She satisfied her by putting a letter of the Alphabet on the black board each morning and has them say it a few times. They all seem interested." Then Kendra glanced at her watch and said, "I do have to run. I don't have much time between Betsy's and my schools," and they both laughed as she hurried out.

The next time she dropped in, Millie asked her how her tenant was working out.

"It's just fine and everything is working out well. We seem to go and come at different times and there are no problems at all."

"I have never seen her, you know. Is she young? old? tall? short? What does she look like?"

"Oh dear, I'm not good at describing people. I think taller than I--oh yes, surely taller. It's hard to tell when sitting down, and I would say a bit over-weight. She did mention that she wanted to lose a few pounds."

"As fat as I am?" asked her mother.

"Oh Mother, No. I...I mean...No." They both started laughing.

"Well Belle is fatter than I am," said her mother, with a laugh, "but go on. Tell me more about your tenant."

"She has short, dark reddish hair and wears rimless glasses, has a very soft voice, much like Miss Heally's whispery voice. Remember my teacher in the lower grades? Miss Branish could be..." She thought for a moment, "maybe sixty. I'm really not very good at describing anyone or guessing ages. Maybe not that old--or maybe older. She seems nice and is no problem. It's working out for all of us."

"Do you see much of her?"

"Not really. Our lives and hours are so different and we don't have much in common. I know nothing about a writing career and I doubt if she knows much about teaching classes."

"But you do see her once in a while?"

"Of course, Mom. We live in the same house and use the same entrance. Miss Branish told me when she first came that she preferred to clean her own room and bath, so there isn't much need for contact. Once a week I leave clean bedding and towels on that little bench outside her door and pick up the used ones later. I asked her about her personal laundry and told her I could do it or, if she preferred, she could come down and use the washer and dryer any time. She said she was used to doing some of her laundry by hand and when she did the balance, she could go to the laundromat near the "Open Door Restaurant." It would work out fine as she was going to get one of those little roller carts, and she could eat at one of the near-by restaurants or do some shopping while she waits for the laundry."

"You don't really see her much at all do you?"

"No, I think she is pretty dedicated to her work, and unless she was going out she wouldn't have a reason to come down--unless something was wrong. I certainly hope everything is fine. If she were on her way out and I was there, then of course we would visit a few minutes."

"If she was on her way out and if you were there, but that has never happened has it?"

"No, I don't believe so."

"So she never goes out when you are home?"

"I guess she hasn't yet. She has only been here a few weeks Mother. We go and come at different times. That's the way it is when we have different types of work."

"Or maybe she is trying to avoid you?"

"Oh Mother, she may be shy, she may sleep late and then work later at night. I was home early a couple of days ago as we got through early from our councilor's meeting, and I knocked lightly on her door. I wanted to see if she'd like to come down and join me for coffee and scones. She was either out or didn't hear me. She hadn't come in when

I had to leave to pick up Betsy so she must have been in her room and didn't hear me. She could have been napping or intent on one of her novels. It's probably not a good idea anyway to interrupt a writer. I wanted her to feel welcome. I did see her a couple of times at the subway entrance when I was driving by, and of course occasionally in the house. For the most part we seem to come and go at different times."

Kendra and her mother decided Miss Branish must be quite a private person who kept diligently to her writing, but her mother wondered about anyone wanting to be quite that private.

"There really is no reason for you to keep the cottage," her mother said to Kendra one day. "You know I have plenty of room and it would cost you nothing to live here, and it would be so handy for you to go to work and leave Betsy asleep in her bed right here. You would save a lot of time if you didn't have to get her up and take her to 'Toddler Town' or bring her to me, and it would be much better for her not to be dragged out of bed so early, and you know I'd love...."

"Mother," Kendra finally interrupted after nervously tapping her toe while she listened, "I know it makes sense for all of us, but you do understand why I want to be on my own don't you? It's all settled and it's working fine.

"Yes, I do understand, and I know I felt the same way when I was young. I guess it's also that things are different now-- more crime for one thing--and Oh, a lot of things like more people, more traffic, and living in this dot-com world makes it more complicated. It seems as though it would be better all..." Her mother interrupted by saying, "Don't worry so much, Mom. Everything will work out fine. You'll see."

Several weeks later Millie Houston's neighbor, Pauline, called her to ask her over for coffee and brownies. "Brownies sound wonderful," said Millie, and they were soon sitting in the cozy den and visiting.

"How is Kendra doing now?" asked Pauline.

"Just fine. She says everything is working out well with her tenant. I'm a little concerned as we don't know anything about her, and no one else seems to have heard of her."

"Well, she does seem strange," said Pauline.

"You know her? You've met her?"

"I don't know her, but I have seen her and knew she was Kendra's tenant. I saw her coming out of the Methodist Church one afternoon. I had forgotten my watch and asked the lady if she had the time. She mumbled something so low that I couldn't understand her then she hurried off. She seemed nervous and embarrassed, and she either hadn't wanted to be seen or was in a big hurry."

"How did you know that she was Kendra's tenant?"

"You remember that my son, Michael lives across the street from Kendra and he has seen the woman. She came into the Palace for dinner a couple of nights ago, and he pointed her out to me." Michael said the woman had come in several times and always asked for the same corner table, and sat almost facing the wall. I have also seen her a few times at, or near, the subway entrance on Brandywine Street when I was going to pick up my grandkids."

"Well you have seen more of her than I have. I have never met the woman," said Millie.

"You probably will soon." Then she said excitedly, "Did I tell you about Michael's plans to build onto the Palace?"

"No," said Millie, still thinking about what Pauline had told her about Kendra's tenant.

Pauline proceeded to tell her all about the new plans for her son's restaurant, but Millie had been thinking only of what she had said about Kendra's tenant. When she had said she had seemed embarrassed as though she didn't want anyone to see her, Millie thought that sounded like the woman all right--so did sitting where she would be the least conspicuous. What was wrong with the lady that she didn't want to be seen or talk with anyone? What was she up to?

About a week later, she had asked Kendra if her tenant was as elusive as ever. Kendra had told her that she hadn't seen her for a couple of weeks.

"Are you sure she is still there?" asked her mother.

"Oh yes," Kendra laughed and told her that each week her bedding was outside on the bench and the fresh bedding had disappeared.

Millie couldn't get that woman out of her mind and she intended to find out anything she could about this stranger living in her daughter's house.

Millie knew she needed help on this, so called each of her Bid Whist friends and set up a special time for one of their game days.

The four women, Belle, Mable, Kate, and Millie, had been friends since the first grade of school and met periodically to play Bid Whist and talk over their lives and problems. They had continued to live in the area since going through school together and were almost as close as sisters. Belle used to be a school principal and seemed to think she should be the instigator of whatever they did. After all those years the others accepted this. They were all in their late seventies and Millie, Kate, and Belle were rather chubby--Belle being the chubbiest of all, and Mable was the thin one. Those four ladies had helped each other with many problems, especially in the years since they had each lost her husband. They had also helped each other through other bad times.

Millie had everything ready for their meeting and plopped into her recliner to wait for them. Her phone rang and she quickly picked it up, hoping it wasn't one of her friends who couldn't make it. She relaxed when it turned out to be a woman taking a survey of sorts. When she asked Millie if she could take a minute or two of her time for a survey. Millie remembered that miserable time years ago when she couldn't get work and had gone door to door taking a survey for the Homer Slater Company, and felt sorry for the lady. "Yes, if it can be short as I'm expecting company," she said. The woman asked about what appliances she had, what brand, etc. She sounded young and had a nice soft voice. Millie was glad to help her and it had been short as promised. She had almost told her she was too busy but was glad she hadn't as she remembered having doors slammed in her face years ago. It would probably feel the same to have someone click off the phone.

When her friends had all arrived at Millie's house and were seated comfortably in the living room Millie explained, "I am very concerned about Kendra's tenant as she seems too much of a loner to be real. I don't know much about the woman--just enough to be suspicious. She doesn't seem to want to talk with anyone and keeps away from everyone, even Kendra."

"Have you met her?" asked Belle.

"No I haven't, but Pauline told me that when the woman comes into The Palace for dinner sometimes, she always asks for a corner table and sits almost facing the wall. It's as though she really doesn't want to see or talk with anyone," said Millie, "and she told me later that she also comes in when the restaurant opens or very soon after. That way she leaves before the crowds start coming. That sounds as though she wanted to leave before many people could see her."

"Well," said Belle, "Since she has never seen any of us, if we could get a look at her we could kind of watch her, couldn't we? Maybe we could take turns, sort of following her until we find out her favorite restaurant, then plan lunch at that restaurant to see if she meets anyone--that sort of thing. Do you think she is some kind of a criminal?" she asked Millie.

"I'm beginning to wonder about it. She is so obviously unfriendly and goes out of her way to avoid people. Kendra told me she had seen this Branish woman a couple of times at the subway entrance, and Pauline had also mentioned seeing her there a few times. It appears she must go often. I don't know if I told any of you but Pauline met her coming out of the church on Spanny Street one afternoon and asked her for the time, and she mumbled something and hurried off. Pauline said she acted embarrassed as though she didn't want to be seen."

"Doesn't Pauline's son live across from Kendra?" asked Kate. At Millie's nod, she said, "Well let's get busy. Maybe we could go by twos. It seems as though that would be more comfortable and less conspicuous seeing two people visiting and looking around and in store windows instead of one person following her."

Millie said, "All I have for a description is what Kendra told me. She is taller than Kendra, wears dark clothing, and rimless granny glasses, and has quite short blunt-cut dark red hair. I don't remember what else she told me. Oh yes, she's not as fat as I am." They all laughed, then Millie added, "She said the lady wanted to lose a few pounds."

"A few pounds? No, I would say she's not as.... plump as you are," said Belle laughing. Then they were all laughing.

Mable asked, "If this lady is so afraid of being seen and so secretive why does she eat out in restaurants?"

"She only has a room and bath," said Millie, "and no way to cook. She told Kendra when she first saw her that she didn't like to cook anyway, so preferred eating out."

Mable said, "Then I suppose she must go to different restaurants so it would be hard to determine which ones we might find her in. We would have to follow her.

It was finally agreed that Millie and Kate, since they lived so near each other, would start by going to the subway station, as the woman had been seen there several times, then they would report to Belle and Mable. Since Mable and Kate did still drive some, they would make a point of going by Kendra's house as well as the subway entrance whenever they were out on an errand. They might catch sight of someone fitting that description. And Mable would talk to people and try to find someone who knew her or knew something about her.

"There has to be someone who knows that woman," said Millie.

They played a few hands of Bid Whist while there, then Millie served them sandwiches, coffee, and cup cakes.

Kate phoned Millie the day they had planned to go to the Brandywine subway station to find out the best time to leave.

"If she goes out to lunch, how about planning to get there about 11:30?" said Millie. "I could call Handy Harry, or we could walk."

"Should we call him? We want this to be quiet don't we? But I don't think you feel like walking."

"I really do, so if you do too, let's go this morning. If you don't want to walk we can call another cab company, although I doubt if Harry would ever mention it to anyone."

Kate came over about 10:00 since they weren't sure how long it would take them. The two of them, armed only with Kendra's description of Miss Branish, walked slowly to the subway entrance, which was much farther than Millie had realized.

By the time they arrived at the subway station, Millie was so tired she didn't think she felt like waiting to see if Miss Branish was coming. They did, however, lumber down the stairs single file. After a short wait, they were ready to leave when the two people, sitting on the one small bench, got up. Kate hurried over to the bench to reserve it and Millie got there and plunked down beside her. Kate shoved over slightly and they both had one leg over the edge since there were no arms on the bench. Millie was wondering how she would get up off that bench, and Kate was thinking this was a crazy thing to be doing. There had to be some easier way to find out about Kendra's tenant.

After two subway trains had come and gone, and no sign of anyone resembling Kendra's tenant, they decided to go home. Kate got up and helped Millie to her feet and they climbed the stairs. Once outside they entered a nearby cafe and had a leisurely lunch, then found a cab to go home.

Once inside Millie's living room Kate said, "Do you want to try it again when we're rested? I really don't mind. Are you busy tomorrow? We can call a cab."

"Now that I'm rested, it's beginning to look more doable, and I have no plans for tomorrow. Today probably wasn't her day. And yes, I do want to call a cab next time."

The next day around 11:00 Millie called a cab, and they arrived at the subway station at about 11:15. As they were starting down the stairs Kate said, "If we cross the street and go into Presby's drug store we should be able to see up the street."

"A good idea," replied Millie, and they crossed and entered to find the best spot. Millie looked longingly at the counter stools but knew they wouldn't have a very good view from there, and people would be getting in front of them. Noting the rotating stand of post cards, they found they could see clearly from there and stood by it, turning it occasionally. They appeared to be looking through the cards as they kept watch out the window.

"Why is the traffic stopping?" asked Millie a little later. That high van is right in front of us and we can't see across the street now."

"Oh no," said Kate, "I forgot about that traffic light. Do you realize we crossed right there and never even thought that cars would be stopping?" The cars started up again and they both breathed a sigh of relief. "Anyway," added Kate, "we probably wouldn't have another high one like that right in front of us and that wasn't a long light." They again had a clear view across the street.

After waiting a while longer with cars stopping at intervals, they decided to forget the whole thing and have some lunch somewhere.

"She may have already come when our view was obstructed," said Millie, "or more likely this wasn't a day she was coming."

Suddenly as the cars were again slowing for that light and Millie had already turned to leave, Kate spied someone who matched the description of Miss Branish. She had definitely come from the direction of Kendra's street. She was wearing a dark outfit and the sun was glinting on her glasses. "Millie wait!" called Kate. "Look, could that be her? It matches the description Kendra gave you--dark short hair and glasses and..."

"It could be, it could be," she said in excitement. "come on." The lady was walking with hurried steps toward the subway entrance, as Millie and Kate now moved as fast as Millie could to make it outside and to the walk light. The lady was just far enough away so they were able to get across the street and down the stairs ahead of her. Those two chubby women had to walk single file as they wobbled their way down the stairs to give faster walkers a way to get by them, then they waited off to one side for the subway train. They could see the train coming and as soon as the lady got in the line to enter it they got behind her. Millie collapsed onto a seat, and Kate was right beside her. They were two rows behind the lady, who looked neither right nor left, but straight ahead and spoke to no one. They both had noted that the lady's glasses were indeed rimless.

Millie whispered breathlessly to Kate, "I'm as.... sure ...as I ...can be." She was breathing hard and hoping it would be a long enough ride so she could get her breath back and the ache in her knees would abate a little before she had to move. As she looked at the back of the lady's head, she noted that her hair was sort of a dark maroon color and cut rather short and straight across. Any hair that people had called red had been more of an orangey color. Still the length of it...and Kendra had said it was "dark" red or auburn, or did Millie just think auburn? The glasses--yes, she felt confident that this was Kendra's tenant.

It was not as long a ride as she had hoped for, but when the lady started to rise at the Melbourne exit Millie and Kate were ready and got up to move quickly to the door ahead of her. They stepped to one side after exiting and Millie went through the pretext of searching for something in her pocketbook while they waited for Miss Branish to lead the way. Millie was thinking that she might have been quite good at detective work in her younger days, and her friends had laughed at her for dreaming of such a strange career. She had indeed dreamed of it and was secretly making plans to explore it further, but those plans were all forgotten when her parents bought her the piano. That was the end of any other thoughts or dreams. She knew she wanted to play that piano more than anything else in the world, and had never been sorry for her change in plans. She did occasionally wonder though how.... Kate punched her and she came back to the present. The lady they were following crossed the street to enter the Purple Plum Restaurant, with Kate following her and Millie hobbling painfully after Kate. When the lady entered the restaurant the two friends stopped outside and, standing in front of a menu taped to the glass, pretended to read it as they peered in the window. Millie was trying to catch her breath as they watched.

A young man seated at a table near the back of the restaurant stood up smiling and came around to the front of the table to pull out a chair for the lady. When they were seated they both started laughing, at least Millie and Kate assumed the lady was laughing too as her head went back and her shoulders shook a little. They soon seemed to be having an animated conversation as he appeared to lift up his tie then drop it. They couldn't see him very well with the lady in front of him as the pair continued to laugh.

"A lot of men wear light blue ties, don't they? What was that all about?" asked Kate.

Millie shrugged her shoulders, "Some inside joke maybe. They obviously know each other well. There aren't many people there yet, and no one seems to be looking in their direction."

"You're right," said Kate. "So what do you want to do--go in and get that table near them? She has never seen either of us".

Millie looked distraught, as she replied, "This was kind of a bad idea, wasn't it? At least I feel disgusted with myself, and I hope Kendra never finds out about this little excursion. We have only seen one waitress, who is a complete stranger to us. We can't learn anything about the woman this way."

As she watched she was thinking, so the woman met a young man for lunch, and what of it? And what am I doing on this dreary day standing here watching them with my shoulders aching and my hips and knees about to give out? She, too, had thought fleetingly of going inside, sitting at the table to the right of them and possibly hearing some of their conversation.

Suddenly feeling very guilty, she turned to Kate and said, "I'm sorry I got you into this as I feel like a criminal. The woman has a right to go wherever she wants, and I would hate to have someone following me."

"I think I agree with you," said Kate. "If we knew something definite that she has done wrong...but it is only suspicion, isn't it? The only thing is that we don't know her and she seems too secretive and to be a loner."

Millie added, "And I'll bet at least half of those kinds of people aren't criminals." They both laughed, as they turned at once and started back across the street to the subway entrance.

"If Kendra knew about this," said Millie, "she would think her mother was out of her mind--and she would probably be right." She wondered to herself if she could even make it back as they waited for the next train. Kate put her arm around her and helped her to the entrance, knowing how much she was hurting and said, "Kendra won't learn of this from Belle, Mable, or me. I'm sure you know that, so don't think about it."

"Thank you," said Millie to her friend. "Yes, I really did know that." She was relieved, out of breath, and hurting all over when she got back to the Brandywine subway stop. They followed the crowd out of the train but stood to one side until everyone had gone ahead of them both up and down the stairs. Millie could step with one foot, then bringing the other up to it while clinging to the rail, as Kate carried her bag, until she arrived at street level.

"Let's go in here," said Kate. I know they have a bench where we can rest for a bit, then we'll get a cab," and she led Millie into the nearest store, which featured art supplies. There were displays of paintings hanging on the walls, and a young couple was admiring one of the pictures. The clerk was helping a woman with supplies, and a quick look around told Millie there was no one in the store who knew her. They joined a dozing gentleman on a wooden bench by the entrance until they were both breathing easier and the ache in Millie's knees had subsided a little.

"We'll wait until you are rested, then get a cab," said Kate.

"I'll bet you are as tired as I am," said Millie.

"I'm a little tired, I admit, but my hurts aren't in my hips, so aren't aggravated by walking like yours are. We'll try and get some information about Kendra's tenant some other way."

"I know if I could lose some weight it would help," said Millie. "I should join a class somewhere as I can't do it alone."

"And Belle and I should too, but we couldn't leave Mable out and you know we four always do those things together, so it's impossible isn't it?"

Millie was still laughing as she said, "We've got to fatten her up so she can join us in a diet plan."

Actually none of them were too concerned about their weight except as it might effect their health. They were beyond worrying about their looks to that extent. Kate had said once, "My mother used to say, 'My kids may not be beautiful but they're clean'." They rested a short while longer, and then looked out the revolving glass door to make sure there was no one in sight who might recognize them. A cab was approaching as they went out, and they hailed it for a ride, both thankful as there was no way Millie could have walked back.

When they arrived at Millie's house, Kate went inside with her to make sure she would be all right. "You will rest now, won't you?" asked Kate, then quickly, "We didn't have lunch. I'll go over and make some sand...."

"No, I've got plenty right here. Let's rest a few minutes, then we'll get something here."

"If you prefer, but I'm really not that tired. The ride home was enough to rest me, and I can make a couple of sandwiches for us."

Millie told her what she had in the refrigerator and, they decided on chicken-a-la-king. After making their decisions, it was only minutes until Kate returned with a tray for Millie. "Microwave ovens are wonderful. Why don't you eat right where you are, and use the end table for your tea, and I'll use the coffee table. This is nice."

Later when they had finished dessert of cookies and ice cream and Kate had washed the few dishes, she said, "We may as well eat while we can. We'll be starting that diet as soon as we get Mable fattened up," and they were both laughing.

"I'm very grateful to you for trying to help me," said Millie later, "but unless we have some proof of something more criminal than wanting to be alone I sure don't want to do anything like that again."

"Whatever you want. You know we are here to help when you need us."

The two friends visited for a while longer, then Kate left for home.

Millie stayed right where she was for over an hour, and she vowed never to do anything like that again. She also knew that she would never tell Kendra, or anyone else, what she had done. She knew her three Bid Whist friends would keep her secret. She couldn't stop worrying about that tenant though. She felt sure that something about the lady was not right. She felt that most people that secretive had something to hide, and she wondered what Miss Branish was hiding. Then she realized that instead of having no friends, she had met one for lunch today, so why am I still thinking something is wrong?

One day when Betsy was staying with her grandmother until evening, she was looking at a book with her grandmother. She exclaimed as she pointed at a picture, "She looks like the lady upstairs."

"Oh, do you see the lady sometimes?" asked her grandmother. She noted that the picture showed that she had short hair of rather odd color, but other than that it didn't look much like the lady they had followed that morning. Could they have made a mistake? She finally decided that it was the short hair, as not many people she knew had hair cut blunt and that short. The lady in the picture was not wearing glasses either, and her grandmother asked her if the lady upstairs wore glasses. Betsy said she didn't think so.

Betsy then said, "One time when Mommy went over to Maxwell's she let me stay home. The lady came out of her room with some sheets. She looked down the stairs and stopped quick when she saw me and said she thought I went out. I told her just Mommy went over to get milk, and the lady went back in her room."

"That's the only time you've seen her?" hers grandmother asked.

"I don't see her in the house. Sometimes I see her at night when I'm looking out my window. Mommy comes in to say good night to me, and then goes to bed. I like to watch the lights out the window for a little while when they go blinky blink." "Does the lady go out a lot at night? And does your mother know that?"

"No. I watch the lights blink, and see the lady go out, but I don't stay very long, then I go to bed. You won't tell Mommy, will you?"

"Don't you think you should tell her?"

"It's okay if the lady goes out isn't it?"

"Yes, I didn't mean... Of course it's all right. I guess it doesn't matter as long as you go to sleep very soon."

Now Millie Houston had another worry. Why was this woman going out so much at night, especially after Kendra and Betsy had gone to bed? It certainly seemed as though she didn't want Kendra to know she went out, or didn't want to talk with her. After giving it a lot of thought she decided Betsy was right. It's okay if she goes out. After all she did live there, paid rent, and had a key--and it's not anyone's business when or where she goes. But she did seem to deliberately keep out of Kendra's way--and she couldn't help but wonder why.

Later she asked her daughter what she really knew about this stranger who lived with them.

"She's a woman who needed a room to do her writing. It's true that I don't see much of her but we manage. I leave the linens and towels, she leaves the used ones, and she leaves the rent each month in an envelope and...."

"In an envelope?" she exclaimed. "Does she pay you in cash?"

"Yes. Some people do. I understand it's still perfectly legal," and she laughed at her mother's concern.

"But why not pay by check as most people would, so she would have the check for a receipt? Doesn't that seem strange to you?"

"I really hadn't thought about it. I leave her a receipt the next day and it works out fine. In fact it saves me from going to the bank as often. She might not even have a checking account. I doubt that everyone has one. They all manage their money the way they prefer. They could use money orders or pay in cash."

"But just leaving cash on a bench doesn't make sense to me," said her mother.

Kendra laughed and said, "Oh Mom, It's the way she prefers to do it, and it's fine with me. You don't like her, do you mother?"

"Like her? You forget that I haven't even met her although I'm your mother and live only two streets away. Why haven't I met her?"

"There's so little free time for all of us, and it never occurred to me that you would be that interested. If you really want to meet her I'll arrange something soon." "But you told me once that your paths rarely cross."

"Well I don't like to disturb her as she could be writing, napping, or making notes for her books, but I could leave a note and...."

"No no, of course not. She obviously doesn't want to be talked to or even seen, but I guess writers are usually a little eccentric, aren't they?"

Kendra laughed and said, "Mother, I think you read far too many of those "Whodunnit" things. Have you ever thought of taking up writing yourself? I think it would be a natural for you. I'm sure you could come up with lots of plots." Her mother laughed too and changed the subject, but she was still more than uncomfortable about the whole set-up. She was very worried about her daughter and granddaughter living with a stranger.

One evening she was talking with Kendra over the phone and asked her where Miss Branish had lived before coming to this area. She was shocked when Kendra told her she thought it was either in this town, or near here, as she seemed to know the restaurants, theaters and shopping areas.

"But you don't know?" exclaimed her mother. "Didn't the references...? You did get references didn't you?"

Kendra hesitated then said, "I was thinking of that the other day and realized I hadn't. I had never lived in an apartment and never rented to anyone, and I just didn't think of it. I guess it was foolish, but one of our substitutes, Miss Clarmont, had told me her neighbor of many years had recommended her. You're right, Mom. In retrospect I should have, but it would be a little awkward now to ask for them. Anyway everything is working out fine and she seems nice enough--busy like all of us. I was thinking I would ask Miss Clarmont a few questions about her, and I will, Mother. I'm sure it will make you feel better."

Millie was thinking of this conversation much later when she was on her way for her yearly two-week reunion with her two sisters. She was glad her daughter was going to try and get more information about her tenant, and decided she would not worry about Kendra and Betsy and enjoy her visit. After all her daughter was a grown-up now and an exceptionally intelligent person.

CHAPTER 3

When Millie returned after a wonderful visit with her sisters, Kendra was waiting for her at the airport. She felt such a rush of pride and love for this beautiful daughter of hers. As they hugged, Kendra told her, "Mother, your sisters are like a shot in the arm for you. You look great, but I'll bet you're tired after that long flight."

"I am a little tired, but we did have a lovely time."

"It was just what you needed, Mom, to get your worries off from us. Aunt Bess and Aunt Gerty sounded good over the phone. How are they really?"

"As spry as ever it seemed to me, and I had trouble keeping up with them at first."

"Well you are a little older and you also have arthritis, which can slow anyone down. I hope you didn't do too much."

"Oh no, they slowed down for me, and we all had a wonderful time reminiscing, but I did miss you and Betsy and was concerned about you."

"We're doing great, Mom. Don't worry about us."

"You certainly sound as though you were. Is that strange renter still with you?"

"She's not strange any more than I am, Mom. We have nothing in common, are both busy, and seem to come and go at different times. I talked with our substitute, Pearl Clarmont, and she said her neighbor, Mrs. Richards, was away visiting, so I couldn't talk with her myself. She had assured Pearl that she would have no second thoughts about renting to Miss Branish herself if she had a second bathroom. That satisfied me."

Her mother breathed a sigh of relief. "Then I do feel much better," she said.

They picked up Betsy from "Toddler Town" then hurried to her grandmother's house where Kendra had started the dinner earlier. When they arrived Kendra told her mother to sit down and relax while she finished preparing their meal. She even had the place settings already on the table. Betsy couldn't wait to tell her grandmother all they had done while she was gone. She had talked fast trying not to leave out anything on their drive over to her grandmother's house, and she excitedly continued after they arrived.

Betsy hurried on, "Mrs. Druise put a star on my tree, and she read a story to us and....," then interrupting herself said in excitement, "and do you know what? Today I passed out the cookies at snack time. That was fun. It was Burton's turn, but Mrs. Druise said he was too 'oopsy,' so she let me do it."

"I don't think I know that word," said her grandmother. "What does 'oopsy' mean?"

"Oh Grammy, you know. It means when someone drops things or bumps into something and says 'oops' then he is being oopsy, and Burton had three oops before cookie time."

Kendra had finished putting their dinner on the table and she laughed and said, "You just taught both Grammy and me a new word. If I said 'darn' when I bumped something would I still be 'oopsy,' or would I have to say 'oops'?"

"I think you have to say 'oops'," said Betsy slowly and thoughtfully, to her mother's and grandmother's amusement. She took her place at the table and soon continued her monologue to her grandmother until her mother told her that Grammy was tired and she had better save the rest until tomorrow. After dinner Millie realized herself how exhausted she was as she kept dozing in her chair.

"You go right along now and get ready for bed," said Kendra. "Betsy and I will take care of things in the kitchen, then we'll lock up and go home. I'll call you tomorrow."

Her mother got ready for bed, not even glancing at her latest mystery book on the bedside table. When she crawled into bed, she was asleep in minutes. Later she half woke up as she heard the car leave, then immediately another car left. She wondered about the second car but was so sleepy that she was soon asleep again.

The following morning she awoke refreshed and got some breakfast from the supplies Kendra had got for her homecoming. About 10:30 Kendra's call came, and after she told her daughter she was completely rested, she asked her if it would be convenient to bring Betsy over for lunch. They both laughed when she told Kendra that she knew Betsy had more to tell her.

Kendra told her mother, "I can't bring her for lunch today as they are having a special birthday party for one of her little classmates. If you aren't busy later it would help a lot if I could bring her over for a couple of hours then. I'll be there as soon as I can make it after I get through at 3:00.

"Of course, that would be fine. Could you stay for a while too?"

"I'd love to, Mom, but I have an appointment with a friend. I shouldn't be longer than about 5:00 at the latest."

"Take all of the time you need, dear. Oh, who came to the house last night? Anyone I know?"

"No, not yet. We hoped we didn't wake you. He's the friend I'm meeting this afternoon, so you'll meet him soon."

Him? her mother thought, I wonder who he can be.

Kendra dropped Betsy off later, kissed them both, and hurriedly left.

About 4:30 Kendra and her friend arrived. He was a handsome young man and quite pleasant. Kendra introduced him as Andy Miller. Betsy ran to him at once and said, "Andy, Isn't my Grammy pretty?"

"She surely is, Betsy. You were right. Did you two have a good time today?"

"We always have a good time, don't we, Grammy?"

"Yes, we certainly do," her grandmother replied absently as she surveyed the young man. Then she asked, "Have we met before? You look familiar."

"I don't think so. I'd surely remember if we had," he replied, as he faced her and smiled.

She thought at first that she might have seen him in a bank, post office, or some other place of business. Then it suddenly came to her--she remembered that smile when he had stood up to greet Kendra's tenant, Miss Branish, in the restaurant the day she and Kate had tried to play detective. She turned away in embarrassment. So that's why he looked familiar. Her mind immediately went into overdrive. How did he know two people, Kendra and Miss Branish, who had so little in common that they rarely met although living in the same house? Had he deliberately sought out Kendra--and for what reason? How long had she known him? What was going on here? When the three of them left with Betsy holding Andy's hand, Millie Houston felt a chill go down her back.

CHAPTER 4

Millie could think of nothing else for the rest of the afternoon and evening, and she decided she needed help and would call her Bid Whist friends in the morning. After thinking it over, she decided she would wait until she had talked with Kendra the next day. Maybe there was an explanation and she shouldn't always think the worst. That night she turned on the local news as usual but couldn't seem to keep her mind on it. It was always so morbid. A car jacking had happened tonight not far from their town. A man and a woman had forced a young student from his car at gun point and driven off in it. The next news item was a woman who had been arrested after she had exited the plane with drugs hidden in the false bottom of a brief case. If it hadn't been for the dogs at this airport she would probably have gotten away with it. Millie felt very uncomfortable that a variety of crimes had been happening so close to home, and wished again that Kendra and Betsy would move in with her so they would at least be together. She sort of watched a game show while her mind raced. She knew the police were doing a good job, and she shouldn't worry so much about her family.

When Millie awoke the next morning her mind went instantly back to the friend of Kendra's. Who was he and what did he want from her? Was Kendra aware that he knows her tenant? When her daughter called, she asked her where she had met Andy.

"He's one of the instructors in the acting class right here at the Rainbow school." Millie felt instant relief. Kendra must have known him quite a while then. Kendra was saying," You mentioned that he looked familiar and it could be that you had seen him on the stage when you and Dad used to go to those Friday night plays. He was very good but he didn't like the discipline of the stage and is much happier instructing. He's a great addition to our faculty and...."

"Addition? Do you mean he has just joined you?" her mother asked in alarm.

"Yes, about a month ago he moved to this school district. I have forgotten where he said he was before, but we are glad he transferred to the Mayland district. He is just what we needed in our acting class. How did you like him, Mom?"

"I don't know him, dear. I have only met him and don't know any more about him than I do about your secretive tenant."

Kendra took a deep breath and didn't bother to answer that and changed the subject to going out to an early dinner some Friday night.

After their visit, her mother was thinking that Andy had moved to this area and had immediately introduced himself to Kendra. She wanted to tell Kendra that she had seen her friend Andy with her tenant, but she couldn't tell her without admitting that she and Kate had seen them together at that restaurant. What reason would they have for being there? They would never have gone to a restaurant far away, and could think of no reason. Of course Millie wasn't supposed to have even seen her daughter's tenant. She knew something was wrong and she wanted to know if this Andy was going to get Kendra into some kind of trouble. Why did he happen to move here recently, then almost immediately get acquainted with Kendra? She owned the very house where the lady had recently rented a room. There had to be a connection that couldn't be good.

Betsy was visiting her grandmother the next day so Millie waited to see her before calling her bid-whist friends. She pulled Betsy up in her lap to read to her, and then instead asked, "Do you like Andy?"

"Umm, he's nice."

"Does he come to your house?" she asked next.

"I don't know. I don't think so."

"How do you see him then?"

"Mommy and I go where he is, then go to a restaurant or to his house. I like to go to his house so I can play with Patty."

"Who's Patty?"

"Andy's little girl. I'm a little bit under Patty but Mommy said I'm almost one whole inch taller."

"You mean you are a little bit younger than Patty?"

"Yes, I am, but only a little."

"Do you like her mother?"

"I don't think Patty has a mother. A Mrs. Gold-something stays with her when Andy is gone. Sometimes I stay with Patty when Andy and Mommy go somewhere."

Suddenly guilt washed over her grandmother, and she picked up the book and said, "Well, shall we read?" but her mind was busy as usual trying to figure out what was going on. Betsy cuddled down happily to listen to the story.

Later, while Betsy was picking out more books, Millie called Kate and told her briefly what she had discovered.

"You're positive he's the one we saw with Kendra's tenant?"

"Oh yes, it was definitely him. He was even wearing a light blue tie. That could have been the same one he was wearing when we saw him. There was nothing laughable about it that I could see. But will you please set up another Bid Whist meeting as soon as you can? We do have something definite now, and I'm so worried," she whispered, "about Kendra and Betsy, not knowing what her tenant and that man are up to. I'm afraid Kendra is walking into something dangerous."

As soon as Kendra had come for Betsy and they had left, Millie called Kate and asked, "Did you tell Belle and Mable everything?"

"I did, and they are both very concerned too and we all want to help in any way we can. Can you come here tomorrow afternoon?"

"Oh, thank you Kate. The usual time? I'll be there."

As soon as the four friends had gathered at Kate's house, no one even thought of their game of Bid Whist. Belle got out the notes she had made and read them aloud with everything up to date including this last revelation of Kendra's young man being the one who met her tenant in the restaurant. Then she started asking the questions that she had also written down. "Who is he? Where did he come from? What is this tenant to him? What does he want from Kendra? Should Millie tell Kendra?"

"No," shouted Millie. "I certainly can't tell Kendra that I followed her tenant, or that I was even at that restaurant."

"But how else could we possibly know that they know each other and met for lunch?" asked Belle.

"Believe me, I would tell her," said Millie almost in tears, "if I didn't know that she would call it my overworked imagination."

"We've got to start asking questions," offered Mable, "and maybe even following both of them until one of us might accidentally see them together in a place where we might be apt to go, at least once in a while."

"But what are the chances of that happening?" asked Kate.

"If she eats out for all, or most of her meals," said Belle, "she is bound to occasionally go to a restaurant in our area and would maybe meet him there. She doesn't have a car so can't go too far from Maison Street. We have to go out more until one of us sees something, and I would have no qualms about following either one if I knew what they looked like. Millie, you will have to give us a better description of Kendra's friend, Andy. Since we feel that Kendra or Betsy might be in danger, we'll do whatever it takes."

"Thank you all," said Millie. "I think we have reason to follow them now, but when Kate and I followed Miss Branish we didn't really have a good reason, just a feeling."

Millie gave as good a description of Andy as she could remember--quite tall, blue eyes, dark hair with a conventional cut, combed back, nice looking, rather on the thin side, with a square chin."

They did end up playing a few hands of Bid Whist, but they were each planning her strategy to find out more about those two mysterious people.

Millie started taking a lot more walks than usual and several times had actually told Kendra that she would not be available on a particular day to keep Betsy, or changed the time so she could get her walk at lunch time. Her three Bid Whist friends were doing the same.

A couple of weeks later when Betsy was again visiting her grandmother, she told her that she had stayed with Patty and Mrs. Goldfield for the weekend and her mother and Andy went somewhere. She apparently had a wonderful time, as Mrs. Goldfield had taken them shopping and bought them identical dresses. Her grandmother could only wonder about her daughter and granddaughter spending so much time at this young man's house. Why was Kendra with him so much and letting Betsy spend so much time with his daughter? And the biggest question was, why, if he knew both the tenant and Kendra, didn't he go to her house? Why had he contacted her, and what was she getting involved in? Betsy interrupted her thoughts with, "You know what, Grammy?"

"No, what?" she asked absently.

"One time Mommy and I met Andy and Patty and we all ate in a restaurant. After we got through eating they let Patty and me play in a game room and a lady let us take turns pushing the button to make colored bubbles. That was fun. When you were little did you make colored bubbles?"

"No, dear, I don't recall that I did," and she realized how much time Kendra and Betsy were really spending with this Andy and his daughter.

Later on a day when Betsy was going to stay with her grandmother, Kendra came rushing in with her, and she hadn't looked this animated since Thurm died. Her mother said, "You're always in such a hurry. Can't you sit down for a few minutes before rushing off again?"

She hesitated, glanced at her watch, then said, "For a few minutes Mom," and sat down beside her mother while Betsy went to the toy box.

"Kendra," Millie immediately asked, "what is going on with you and this Andy?"

"Mother, his name is Andrew and he is called 'Andy'--not 'This Andy' and we enjoy each other's company so we get together when we can. What do you mean by 'What is going on?' and why are you so concerned?"

"It seems as though you haven't known him very long and I wondered how much you really know about him."

"It's true. I haven't known him very long, but we have things in common, including little girls about the same age, and we are enjoying getting acquainted. That's the way you find out about people, a little at a time. I'm a big girl, Mother. Don't worry about me. I know what I'm doing so trust me."

"But why doesn't he pick you up at your home instead of meeting you somewhere?"

"Now where did you hear that?" interrupted Kendra, as she stared at her mother in amazement.

"Something you said, I guess," she stammered. "At least that was what...I'm sorry if I got the wrong impression."

Betsy came over at that moment with a game and plunked it in her grandmother's lap. "You said you'd play it with me next time I came," she said, "and this is next time."

As her mother stood up, she said, "But you don't interrupt when people are talking, Betsy. I was just leaving, but next time, remember, won't you? Now be a good girl and do what Grammy says."

"And Mom, stop worrying. Everything is fine."

Her mother didn't think everything was fine, and wondered about Andy as well as the tenant. What wasn't Kendra telling her? She knew she was holding back something. Was she being taken in by this Andy? And for what reason? "Yes, yes, Betsy, we'll take it over to the table and play it."

When Kendra came that night she looked happy and relaxed. Betsy ran to her mother and asked, "Did you tell Patty about the white kitten?"

"Yes, I told her and she thought 'Corky' was a funny name too."

Millie was hurt and thinking that her daughter hadn't told her that she was seeing Patty--and apparently Patty's father--but Betsy knew it.

As she watched Betsy and Kendra pick up the toys she wondered what her daughter would think if she knew her mother had followed her tenant to try to find out something about her. "Did you tell Patty that I would come next time?" Betsy asked her mother.

"No dear, I didn't promise, but told her you would come to see her as soon as we could manage it."

Kendra never again mentioned the remark that her mother had made about Andy not picking her up at her house. In fact she never said much about her life at all, and they had always been so close. Her mother was thankful that Kendra still brought Betsy to her when she felt like having her--but she wished that tenant would move out. She wished she could convince Kendra that the perfect solution would be for them to move in with her and save whatever they netted for the cottage and put it with Thurm's insurance. It would be a guarantee of a college education for Betsy, and more comfortable for her too if she had them living with her. It would certainly be safer for all of them to be together.

One evening after Betsy had spent the day with her grandmother the phone rang and it was Kendra asking her mother if she felt like keeping Betsy overnight. If not, she could pick her up and take her to Andy's house for the night.

"I feel like it," said her mother, "but is something wrong? You sound breathless."

"Oh no, but something has come up and I have to go out. If you're sure you're okay it would help a lot." Kendra quickly thanked her and said good night.

What in the world was going on that was so urgent that she would even think of moving Betsy around like that so she could go out?

As sleepy as Betsy was after her bath, her grandmother sat down by her bed and deliberately kept her awake as she asked her questions. She had never felt so guilty, but she was sure something was awfully wrong and Betsy obviously knew more about what was going on than she did. "Betsy, does Andy come to the house now to pick up your mother?"

"No, Mommy asked him why not, but I don't know what he said."

"Does anyone come to see Miss Branish?" she asked her.

"I don't know. One night I heard Mommy talking to a man in the hall. Maybe he came to see the lady."

"He asked to see someone?"

"I don't know what he said. I could tell a man was talking, then I heard the door shut, and it kind of banged."

She thought about that a minute, then asked, "Has Andy ever sounded angry?"

"I think one time at his house he was 'cause he banged his hand hard on the counter and I went right back upstairs to Patty's and my room."

Oh, so it was Patty's and Betsy's room now, thought her grandmother.

Betsy was saying, "I was going to see if we could have some popcorn but Mommy and Andy both looked like they would say no, so I didn't ask. Patty went down to ask and she came back and said she could tell that her daddy would say no, and she said Mommy looked like she was kind of mad too, but she got us some cookies anyway."

Suddenly her grandmother felt frightened. "Do you know where your mother went today after she left you here?"

"Nope, I don't," she said around a yawn.

Her grandmother quickly said "Time to get some sleep," and she tucked her in, gave her a kiss, and left. She was thinking, Were Kendra and this Andy having an argument? Then maybe she wouldn't continue to see him. Had she found out something about him? Maybe she was going out with someone else tonight, or maybe....No, she thought. This was silly as she couldn't begin to guess what was going on, but she had to find out some way. She didn't want Kendra caught in some trap.

Millie Houston got ready for bed, finished reading the paper, then glanced at the clock. It was time for the 11:00 p.m. news. This seems to be part of my ritual of going to bed, she thought as she listened and watched the first news item. It was a tragic fire that destroyed two apartment houses. At least no one lost their life, and all of the tenants had found places to stay. Three of the firemen and an elderly woman were treated for smoke inhalation, and a lot of people lost their homes and possessions. All of the crime as well as the tragedies make the news, and I watch it before going to bed. No wonder I have trouble getting to sleep, she thought. As always there were break-ins and other crimes, and now a man was caught spying against his own country. What was this world coming to? Suddenly she thought of Miss Branish, could she be a spy too? She tries not to be seen any more than necessary, never goes out of her way to talk with anyone, even her landlady. She has even arranged things so no one else goes near her room and she insisted on getting a lock on her door immediately when she moved in. Why did it have to be immediately when there was only Kendra and a four-year-old girl in the house besides herself. And, according to Betsy, Miss Branish goes out often at night. She met Andy in the restaurant that day and he could easily be an accomplice. While she was supposedly writing her books she could be writing or sorting out the material she had gathered when she went out those nights. She could pass it on to Andy. He could be transferring it to someone who would pass everything on to an enemy country. He must have an ulterior motive to have arranged to work where Kendra does, and he certainly knew that Miss Branish lived in her house if he was meeting the woman for lunch. Millie had to warn Kendra some way. Should she tell her about spying on...Oh dear there was that word connected to herself, and she laughed. Kendra was probably right about her imagination. It was silly to let her mind roam like this. It was only that she knew nothing about Miss Branish or this Andy, but of course that was no reason to assume that they were automatically suspicious characters. But why keep it secret from Kendra that they knew each other? There was a reason for that. She reached for the TV remote, then stopped. They were telling about a young man who had risked his life to save two little children in a fire and the grateful and tearful mother was shown thanking the embarrassed teenager. Millie turned off the television and thought, Yes, there are a lot of good things happening out there, and she was glad this incident had made the news tonight. She needed that and she would try hard to remember that good things happened too, but they were not as likely to make the news as they were more common. She checked the doors once more, and went to bed, feeling much better as she picked up her latest mystery and got ready to figure out who the guilty person was.

CHAPTER 5

A few weeks later Millie Houston was again entertaining her three Bid Whist friends.

They each reported areas where they had been driving or walking and trying to find the two suspects together somewhere. Mable said, "I occasionally have gone to the Mainstream Mall but I have been there four times since the last time we met, and each time after making a right turn onto Spanny Street I stopped in the parking lot of the church and walked back and went inside. The fourth time, as I got to the door, a young man came out and even held the door for me. It might have been the young man you mentioned, Millie, but there was no woman with him."

"She could have gone out first and you missed her," said Kate.

"I thought of that," said Mable, "but I couldn't very well refuse to go in and start looking up and down the street, so I had to enter. The young man had dark hair and was about a head taller than I am. I was close enough to note that he had beautiful blue eyes."

"It sounds like him," said Millie and Kate almost together.

"I'll keep trying," said Mable. "It was about 3:00 p.m. and I'll try that time again, maybe a little earlier and wait inside to see if one or both comes in. Of course all I have is your descriptions of each, but I'm sure if the two of them are together it shouldn't be hard. Isn't that the church where Pauline asked her for the time?"

"Yes, it was," said Millie, "and I expect she was in a hurry to get away before her son, or whoever he is to her, came out. I don't think they want to be seen together."

"Do you think he is her son?" asked Belle.

"It did occur to me as he looks about the right age, but of course I don't know."

None of the others had any luck. They had been talking to anyone they knew, and some they didn't know, trying to find someone who knew, or knew of, Miss Branish.

Millie said, "I really appreciate what all of you are doing and I have a feeling it just might pay off. We're doing all we can. Someone has to know that woman." Then she said, "Now that we are all here we may as well play our game."

Belle suggested Scrabble instead, and they got that game out. They sometimes played other games and didn't mind as long as they were together, but Bid Whist was definitely their favorite. Getting together was habit and whatever they did they all enjoyed. When they got near the end of the game it was Mable's turn and she added the letters `i-n-g' to the word `Spy'. "Ha, triple word," she called.

"Spying pays off", laughed Kate, as she wrote in the score, "and Mable is the winner by about seventy points."

That was all Millie needed to start wondering again if Kendra's tenant was a spy.

Mable said, "Maybe next time it's my turn for our games we can go to the cottage again. They haven't had any break-ins there for three years now and my grandson loves that cottage."

"Did they ever find out who was responsible for those break-ins?" asked Belle.

"Oh yes, some kids in their early teens thinking they were doing something pretty cute. I'm thankful they stopped that. They do grow up eventually."

"I wonder what Kendra's tenant is up to," said Belle. "It's too bad Kendra didn't think to get any references. If we just knew where the woman came from it would certainly help."

"I don't know much about her and I don't think Kendra does either," said Millie. "Knowing nothing about her and with her living in Kendra's house, maybe I do let my mind wander too much. I even wondered at one time if she could be cooperating with a counterfeiter and passing on counterfeit money or doing some real spying."

"You're really concerned about her being some kind of a criminal?" asked Mable.

"There have just been too many of these things that don't add up, like why does she pay her rent to Kendra in cash? And the first thing she did when she rented the room was to ask Kendra if she could have a lock on her door. Of course Kendra had it put on."

"Well that's understandable," said Belle, "as everyone wants to be able to lock their doors, and that's her home for as long as she's renting."

"You're right," said Millie. "It just seemed strange that she wanted it immediately when only Kendra and Betsy were in the house and there are dead bolt locks on the outside doors of the house. Kendra did get it done but had to pay extra for after-hours service, and I'm sure Kendra must have wondered if the woman thought she or Betsy might open her door."

"That is strange. I would have thought she could have waited a day or even two under those circumstances," said Mable. "After all Kendra had just thought of renting that day and wouldn't have had time to do it."

Belle said, "We should see her sometime when we could follow her. I've seen her twice coming out of the house so I would recognize her anywhere."

"Oh yes, she goes out for meals," said Millie.

Belle hesitated then added, "I remember that both times I saw her she was carrying an over-sized tote bag. I wonder if she carries it everywhere she goes."

Millie remembered then that she had been carrying, besides her handbag, a large bag of some kind the day they followed her from the subway. She glanced at Kate, who said, "She was carrying it when we saw her, Millie. And if that young man, Andy, is the one her tenant met in the restaurant that day, Kendra should know about it. What if she really is an agent and she has information that she has to take to someone?"

Belle spoke up. "Girls, girls, let's slow down. I shouldn't have mentioned a tote bag. Almost everyone carries some kind of a bag and it doesn't mean a thing except that we carry way too much stuff around. Changing the subject, we don't even know where the woman came from. It seems to me that is what we should be thinking about. We haven't found anyone so far who ever heard of the lady, so let's set our sights on finding out something about her besides thinking up things that 'might be' without a shred of evidence."

"Belle is right, said Kate, "We do know that Andy moved here from another school district. How can we find out where he moved from? Maybe he came from the same area that Kendra's tenant came from. No one knew anything about her. The woman had only been there a matter of weeks when Andy moved to the area. It surely looks as though it was some kind of a conspiracy, doesn't it?"

"It does to me," said Millie, "and she is living with my daughter and granddaughter."

"I know I'm just surmising, said Kate, "and maybe this person, Miss Branish, is all innocence and charity, but the only family I have ever heard of named Branish was the one over on Canton Street. Remember the trial of Joey Branish. He's still behind bars as far as I know, for robbing the Pantry Mart, and his wife was left with nothing. I think she was washing and ironing clothes for a living."

"But," said Mable, "that doesn't mean she's related..."

"No, of course not, but I'm just saying they are the only other Branishes I've ever heard of, and with an unusual name like that, maybe we should at least check and find out what Miss Branish's first name is and see if she might be related to that family."

"How can that help? Will that make a difference?" asked Mable.

"Maybe not, but it might make a start if we knew where she came from originally. Perhaps right around here, and we could question people who might know her. We know other members of the family, and she could have married someone with that name. So let's keep on the way we are going and we will either find she is related, or at least eliminate that area. Mable seems to be on the right track and who knows, we may come up with something. The only other thing that would help would be for Millie to tell Kendra that we saw that young man with her tenant, and we know she doesn't want to do that."

"And you all know why I can't," said Millie, "She would think I had made a mistake as I haven't seen the woman, as far as she knows," and she left for the kitchen to get the refreshments she had prepared. She soon returned with a large plate of sandwiches and announced, "The coffee is perking", and the other ladies jumped up to help and bring in the cup cakes.

"I'll get the cups, and.... Oh, those sandwiches look yummy." Someone else asked, "Are these cream cheese and olive?" and "Great! My favorites and you rarely see them any more."

"I asked for them one afternoon in Maylons' Cafe," said Kate, "and the waitress said they didn't have them as there wasn't much call for them now. My niece was with me and she told her there might be more call for them if they put them on the menu. I was thinking the same thing, but didn't say anything. Jenny didn't mind telling the woman though."

"That sounds like your Jenny," laughed Mable. "She tells it like it is."

After their refreshments Kate said, "I've been wondering whether I should say anything or not, Millie, but I thought you would want to know. It seemed strange to me when I saw Kendra's tenant last evening near the side of Longman's Restaurant just watching the kids. I knew who she was because of that time we saw her at the Purple Plum."

"What's wrong with watching the children?" asked Belle.

"Maybe nothing, but she was just staring at the children in the game room. Maybe she was watching only one child, who was moving around, but she had a camera and it looked as though she was taking random pictures. We went in and I tried to find a seat where I could see her. She wasn't visible from the inside. I thought she might have left, but when we went out, she was still there. She may have deliberately picked a spot where no one inside could see her. She finally put her camera in her pocket, and just turned and walked away as though in a hurry. When she passed the window it looked to me as though she waved to someone inside. Her free arm was at her side and she just fluttered her fingers up as you might from the steering wheel when driving. I couldn't be positive, but I do think she knew someone inside."

"How strange," said Millie?

"Sandy had wanted to go out in the game room and I told her it was too late. I hadn't known for sure if the woman was still there, but it gave me the creeps seeing her watching and taking pictures of the kids. There were three little ones, two girls and a boy, and I didn't want her staring at my grandchild. After she was out of sight we did go back inside and I let Sandy go in to the game room for a short while. "You're sure that was Kendra's tenant?" asked Milly.

"Oh yes, I'm sure. I got a really good look at her when she came in the Purple Plum one day, and she was carrying the big tote then too. She had it across her lap and her handbag was on the floor. Whatever she had in that large bag seemed to be more important than what she had in her handbag. It sure looked like the bag she was carrying when we followed her."

"About watching the children at Longman's," said Mable, that woman may have lost a child at some time and just likes to watch them."

"Maybe, but I couldn't get it out of my heard that it was something secretive. I didn't know what she had in mind and wondered what she had in that bag. She was so protective of it. She just seems like a strange one to me."

Belle asked, "You are going to tell Kendra, aren't you Millie?"

"But," Mable interrupted, "maybe she just likes to watch children. I know I do."

"But tied in with everything else we've found out, it is just one more thing to wonder about," said Belle, while writing it all down. "Don't you think so Millie?"

"Well yes, I'm sure wondering about it, but what can we do?"

"I didn't know either," said Kate. "I didn't want you to worry, but your Betsy is in the same house with her, and the whole thing looked so odd to me. It's probably nothing to worry about, but I thought I'd at least tell you and let you decide whether to mention it to Kendra."

"It looks odd to me too," said Millie, "in fact more than odd, it's a little frightening. Why take all of those pictures? But if it was her grandchild, maybe. Anyway, Thank you for telling me. I'm not sure what Kendra would make of it." Mable said, "I saw a woman standing out there by the play area one time when I went in for a sandwich, and she was just watching the children. I didn't think anything about it. I assumed she was there to take a picture of her grandchild."

"What did the woman look like?" asked Kate.

"Look like? Just a woman watching the kids." "Usually they go inside if they have children playing there," said Kate. "The children go into the game room from the inside.

"One thing I do remember about this woman," said Mable, "was that she was dressed in dark clothes for such a warm day. Pretty good description isn't it?" They all laughed. Then she said, "I remember now that she was wearing granny glasses as the sun was glinting on them"

"Did she have red hair?" asked Kate excitedly.

"Red hair? I have no idea what her hair looked like. I just remember those hot clothes and the bright sun on her glasses."

"When was it that you saw the woman?"

"Wednesday about noon. I was going home from shopping and decided to stop for a shake to take home to have for my lunch."

"What you have described so far sure sounds like Miss Branish," said Kate. "I'll bet it was, and I wonder why," she glanced at Millie, who looked scared.

Mable looked at Millie's frightened expression too, and said, "Come on, Millie. My goodness if that lady was all of the things you have thought of her, she is one busy lady. You have had her spying with her accomplice, distributing counterfeit money, and what is it this time? Kidnapping children, or breaking into summer cottages?" The friends burst out laughing, and even Millie had to join them.

Mable looked at Millie and realized that she was really worried and she was sorry she had laughed at her fears. She said, kindly, "Millie, don't they say,'Let go, and Let God?' Don't worry so much."

"They also say, 'God helps those who help themselves."

"Well how about letting go of the worrying, and try to help in other ways? Worrying really does no good."

"You're right, Mable. But.... when someone you love might be in harm's way, you are just feeling and not thinking."

When the friends left for home it had been decided that they would each try to think of anything they could do or anyone they could contact who might shed some light on this Miss Branish and come with their notes to the next meeting, or if it seems urgent they would call Millie at once.

Once she was alone, Millie sat down and pushed back the recliner. The more she thought of what Kate had told them, the more it bothered her, but telling Kendra? No, she knew Kendra would find nothing wrong with someone watching children play, but Millie knew it was something else to add to her list. She started thinking about Joey Branish and she remembered the trial. She didn't remember any relatives being mentioned other than his wife, Christy--the poor soul. She realized she didn't even know the first name of Miss Branish, and she wondered if Kendra even knew it. She had said that she always paid her rent in cash--so she wouldn't have seen it on a check. That tenant must have given her first name when she first rented the room. Millie was wondering how she could find out. Of course the simple way would be to ask Kendra, and she decided she would at the first opportunity.

One afternoon when Betsy was with her, Millie casually asked, "Have you seen Miss Branish lately?"

"Nope. She's gone."

"Gone? She's gone?" her grandmother asked, startled.

"Mommy said Miss Branish was away--I think she said `for a bit.' How long is a bit?"

"I'm not sure. Not very long," she answered vaguely. "Did your mother say where she had gone?"

"I don't think so. Can we read the kitten book again?"

"You find it and we'll read it," said her grandmother, but she was wondering why Kendra hadn't at least told her that her tenant was away.

Later when Kendra arrived, her mother said, "Betsy mentioned that Miss Branish was away. Is it permanent, or is she coming back?"

"Oh she'll be back. She paid me in advance and said she had to do some research on a book. Did you and Betsy get out today? It was such a beautiful day."

Her mother told her they had taken a walk to see Mrs. Preston's garden. It was obvious that Kendra didn't want to talk about Miss Branish, or anything else of any substance these days--at least not with her mother. Millie couldn't seem to bring up the subject of the first name of Miss Branish.

The next day Millie was alone and decided to go to the library and do some research of her own. She knew Kate was not working at the library that morning, as her grandchildren were visiting, but she decided to go anyway.

She didn't know the young lady who was taking over, but she helped Millie find the old newspaper printouts for the years she asked for, and Millie eventually found the year of the Joey Branish trial. She read through several issues of that time and found out that Joey Branish had a brother Raymond, and a sister Clara. Even if the first name of Miss Branish were Clara it wouldn't prove she was from the same family--and if she was from that family, it wouldn't prove that she was a criminal like her brother Joey, or that she had been living in the same area. Millie asked the librarian if she would check for an author. She told her she didn't remember the name of the book or the first name of the author, but the last name was Branish. The search turned up no author by that name, but she was told they could have used a pen name.

Millie walked slowly home, bleary-eyed, tired, hungry, and no wiser than when she had started out. Well she did find out that Joey Branish had a sister named Clara. She wanted to find out in some way what was not right about Miss Branish. The fact that this tenant knew Andy, who had only recently made himself known to Kendra, was a real worry. It had to be something underhanded or he would go to the house and see both of them there. They obviously didn't want Kendra to know that they knew each other. What was the reason? She had to find out. Her daughter would never trust her again if she knew her mother had followed her tenant. Could Miss Branish be Andy's mother? She still thought she might be. She surely didn't want to see Kendra get hurt. Didn't Kendra wonder why he didn't pick her up at her house? She had seemed very concerned that her mother knew this, and she must be more concerned about *why* Andy never came to her house. Betsy had said that her mother had asked him why, and Millie wondered what he had answered that Betsy couldn't remember or didn't hear.

About 4:00 o'clock that afternoon Kendra was at her desk at the Rainbow School finishing up some papers when Charlotte, another teacher, tapped on the door, then entered. "Kendra, Mrs. Pentree wasn't very happy about your suggestion of only one or two weeks for the four-year-olds' camping trip. Anyway, I don't think it will fly. We're having a vote tonight to see how many mothers want it. Unfortunately the councilors aren't included in the voting."

"It's all right, Charlotte. Just an idea as I thought four-year-olds were pretty young for the whole three weeks."

"Actually I agree with you," replied Charlotte. "My Tara is three and I can't believe she would be ready for that long a time in just another year. And you knew," her friend added, "that some of the mothers who weren't going would like a three-week vacation from their kids. Right?"

"Right! Free, and willing, baby sitters. We'll get through it. It's also coming at kind of a bad time for me--having a tenant that I don't really know staying in my house alone. Any time I've gone anywhere before this I have locked the door knowing no one would be entering. I have no way of knowing if she is a responsible person who would always lock the door at night or when leaving the house. She probably would since she was so adamant about getting a lock on her door immediately. It's also the first time my mother has been really alone since my Dad died, I mean with Betsy and me being no farther than two streets away. She is worried about Miss Branish and thinks she is some kind of a menace, which doesn't help either."

"How did you find her?" asked Charlotte, as she sat on the edge of Kendra's desk dangling her legs.

"Miss Clarmont came to me and asked if I had a room to rent as her neighbor was looking for a place for a good friend of hers."

"I don't know Pearl Clarmont well," said Charlotte, "but I certainly think she's trustworthy. I wouldn't worry about it."

"I really haven't that many qualms about it either. I guess it's mostly that I wanted some way to reassure my mother that there was nothing to worry about."

Charlotte slid off the desk and said as she headed for the door, "I can understand that it's not really comfortable. Just try to put it out of your mind and try to enjoy your three weeks. Sorry, but I think the vote will be for the entire three weeks."

Kendra thought so too, and after Charlotte left, she sat thinking about her mother being alone when they were gone. She finally realized that her mother was an intelligent woman, her mind seemed fine-- maybe forgetting a word now and then, but who didn't? She did have lots of friends in the area, and since her father had passed away four years ago her mother had seemed to handle her affairs pretty well. If she needed help with anything she knew how and where to get it. She picked up the sheaf of papers and sighed as she started going through them. After a half hour of making notes of the suggestions in them for the volunteers, Kendra decided she would take them home and look through them there. She was glad Betsy was with her grandmother so she could go straight home. She was having trouble keeping her mind on what she was doing. She wished her mother wasn't so worried about her tenant.

While driving home that afternoon Kendra's mind was mostly on her tenant. She had been concerned about her ever since Betsy had mentioned her going out so much at night, and it was always after they had gone to bed. Of course she had a right to go out when she wanted. It was because she knew next to nothing about her. She had been so happy to rent out that little room and be able to send Betsy to "Toddler Town" that she hadn't thought to get the references she should have. It didn't seem right to ask for them now. How could she do it at this late date when Miss Branish was already moved in? Her mother was so concerned about her and, in trying to reassure her, she had raised a few doubts in her own mind. She hadn't known Andy very long but he surely seemed trustworthy and intelligent, and she wondered if she should confide in him. She would certainly give it some thought. She would feel better if she could get his advice. Her mind kept returning to the thought that Miss Branish would be alone in her house while she and Betsy were away, but it couldn't be helped.

One day while Betsy was at her grandmother's house she told her, "Mommy says two more weeks and we can go camping."

"I hope you like it as much as I did when I was little," her grandmother told her. She was thinking that it had been very different back then. There was no camping with a bunch of other children. It was just she and her sisters and their parents, but it was still camping with the swimming, boating, cookouts, and nature walks. What she remembered best was picking berries and the shortcakes their mother made with them. She didn't like thinking of being alone in the house knowing Kendra and Betsy would be nearly two hundred miles away. That was a long way to travel to go camping, but she knew the Bradey Foundation had donated the area to the Rainbow School as well as furnishing the transportation so the cost was still much less than going to a nearer lake. She was worried about that tenant who was a stranger to everyone she knew being in Kendra's house alone. She was reassured though in thinking Pauline's son, Michael, or his wife Corrie, would report anything to Kendra that seemed unusual.

The day came when Kendra and Betsy, all packed to go, had arrived to say goodbye. Millie put on her happy and brave face as she wished them well and told them to have a good time, and she'd see them in three weeks. She assured her daughter that she would be just fine and would keep busy while they were away.

CHAPTER 6

That night Millie listened to the late news as usual. It wasn't always good news, but it was hard to break a habit, especially when she and Kevin used to watch it together, so good or bad, she was there. Watching the news with Kevin hadn't been at all frightening as she always felt safe with him, and he somehow made it entertaining as well. Sometimes the advertisements were a welcome break. Someone might announce that if you call in right now within so many minutes you could save fifty percent off the price, and Kevin would say, "Let's not call in and save one hundred percent." Some of the ads were clever, witty, cute and quite entertaining, but a lot of it was because Kevin was with her. Her mind was on Kevin tonight, as it so often was. This night she went to bed, read a while, and slept.

She awoke the next morning thinking she had got through one night and the rest should go all right too--and everything comes to an end. She straightened up a few things on her way to the kitchen, and then decided she didn't feel like breakfast yet. She absently wandered from room to room and brought in the paper and settled down to read it. She had finished with the news and started on the crypto--trying to keep busy when she heard the whistling. She knew it was Benny Schyler coming with the mail, and went to meet him. "Hello Benny," she said, "How are you this morning?"

"You know me, Mrs. Houston, I'm always okay, and the world's okay too, so don't look so discouraged. Are you all right?"

"Oh my, does it show? Yes, I'm all right, but Kendra and Betsy are away camping, and I guess I'm thinking of all of the crime around."

"But the crime rate is coming down, and a lot of the criminals are being caught, and Kendra and Betsy will be home before you know it."

She sighed, "Yes, of course, and I know Betsy and Kendra will be home soon."

"They sure will and will have a great time. By the way, I saw Kendra last week over on Benton Avenue. Tried to get her attention but a young man was helping her into the car with the driver and she didn't see me. Say hello for me. She looked great."

As he started off he called back, "And something else, Blondie's shoes fit better now. Haven't you noticed?"

Mrs. Houston laughed with him as she thought of that comic strip of Dagwood and Blondie. She went back into the kitchen to fix her breakfast with a lighter heart. So lighten up, Millie, she thought to herself. Benny is right. He always was a cheerful kid and he has a real knack for cheering up others too, and she chuckled again thinking of Blondie's shoes. She was ready by 2:30 and walked across the street to Kate's house to ride with her to Belle's house for their Bid-Whist afternoon.

Millie told Kate about Benny cheering her up that morning. She also told her about his seeing Kendra with two men last week on Benton Ave. "I can't imagine why she would have been over there and with two men? He said she didn't see him."

"Probably one was Andy and the other man was a friend of one of them," said Kate matter-of-factly, which made Millie feel better. "You know they say, 'three's a crowd' and you are always safer in a crowd." Millie laughed with her.

Mable was already there when they arrived at Belle's house. They each reported on the people they had seen and what they had done to try to find out something about Miss Branish. No one seemed to know of that lady. Those who knew Kendra Thermose just knew she had this tenant in her house, but had never heard of Miss Branish in any other connection. According to what Kendra had told her mother, her tenant seemed to know their little suburb very well. It would appear that she might have lived here a while, yet they could find no one who had heard of her. On the other hand, maybe she had moved here recently and just had a good memory for names and places.

Belle said thoughtfully, "It's possible she lived here a while ago and just returned recently. It's a possibility that Branish is her married name and no one would have known it. We have to think of everything."

Mable said, "Yes, we do. Belle and I were wondering before you arrived if you had found out from Kendra where Andy came from."

"No, I haven't. I wish I had asked her when she was confiding in me. Maybe I should just ask her anyway. I was going to and I chickened out."

Belle said suddenly in excitement, "Why don't I go back to the Rainbow School and ask someone, anyone, if they know where he came from? I did used to be the principal there and maybe I could mention that I wondered if he was the son of a certain friend, or something like that. They can't any more than say they don't know or that they can't give out that information. I'll try anyway. That's what I should have done in the first place. I'm sure I can find out, Millie. I know one teacher whose mother was teaching there when I was principal, and I don't mind going over. One of the tactics should work."

"Oh, that would be wonderful," said Millie, "then we should be able to find out something about him, and it's very possible that Miss Branish came from the same area since he knows her."

Mable, said, "If you find out Belle, I'll be glad to pick you up and we can go there and see what we can do."

"Oh, thank you both," said Millie. "I feel much better already. That was the missing link as we never knew where to look for information." She looked around at her wonderful old friends, then said, "Well, now let's not waste this beautiful day and get to our games."

"There wouldn't be any school today anyway," said Belle, so why not play!"

Of course they all loved the game they had enjoyed when their husbands were living, but would have got together anyway just to keep in touch. They used to get together for Bid Whist while their husbands headed for the golf course, then in the winter they had used two tables and the men played with them while alternating partners. None of them, even Belle, took their games seriously now. They all played for the fun of it and for old time's sake--bidding wildly and laughing over the times when they got to visiting and flubbed a play.

After a few games and conversation Belle brought on her fancy refreshments. No one tried to out-do her. It would probably have been impossible anyway and Belle lived to top others. It was just something she loved to do, and no one would try to deprive her of the pleasure. She might be playful with the cards, but she was serious about her refreshments. As they enjoyed the crust-trimmed and fancy-shaped sandwiches, deviled eggs, flakey cream puffs, and coffee, they all did their share of praising the hostess.

They visited longer than usual that afternoon as they got to reminiscing. "Do you know," said Mable, "new friends are nice but there is something about old friends that are especially comforting. I think part of it for us is that we all knew the other husbands."

"I think so too," said Millie. When you mentioned Pete's wild bidding we all remembered it--not just hearing of it, but being there too. It is comfortable isn't it?"

"And our husbands were as good friends as we are," added Belle.

That evening Millie felt better about Kendra and Betsy being gone. After being with her friends and talking about their husbands it was almost as though Kevin was there with her. She listened to the late news while getting ready for bed, and then wished she hadn't; as she found she was too wide awake to sleep. She had felt so comfortable after the visit with her friends that she had automatically turned on the news. She had promised herself she would do as Kendra suggested and not watch the late news--certainly not while she and Betsy were away. Now she had done it again--well, not watched it, but heard some of it--the depressing local news. This was not an inducement to sleep, especially when alone and her family no longer a few streets away.

Kendra had also suggested that her mother give up those detective and suspense novels that she loved so much until they got back. Millie of course realized the news was all about things that really happened, while these books were novels. I can certainly tell the difference, she was thinking. These stories are a pastime and I never think of them once I close the book. There was no way Millie would give up her addictive reading and, settling in Kevin's recliner, she picked up the book she had started and was soon lost in another world. After reading for a long time, she found herself nodding and dropping the book. She switched off the light but was so sleepy that she just closed her eyes and dozed off right where she was.

She was sleeping soundly when something startled her awake. She stared into the darkness, and then realized that she was in the recliner instead of her bed, and peeked out through the gap in the drapes. In the dim haze from a streetlight she saw the shadow of a branch of the lilac bush--or was it? No, it was moving--It was a...No, two forms were coming up her walk. She knew it was late and she was terrified. She leaped up and felt her way past the doorway into the den. Just as she was closing the den door she definitely heard someone trying the front door. She hurried into the closet, closed the sliding door, and then slid through the hanging clothes, sinking to the floor. She stayed cramped on the floor with the corner of something poking into her back--not daring to move, trembling and taking quick shallow breaths, and trying to hear. All of the crimes she had ever heard of came crowding into her head at once as well as all of the warnings she had got since Kevin had died.

The only sounds were the ordinary sounds of traffic, a siren, or an occasional dog barking--all outside noises. She wished she had grabbed her cordless phone. With the door to the den closed as well as the closet door and, with the hanging clothes to further muffle any sound, she heard nothing that could be inside the house. She knew the outside door was locked. Would they try to get in another way or go on to an easier target? Her bed was still made up and if they got in the house it would appear that she wasn't home. She prayed they would not look in the closet if they got in, and she stayed absolutely still for a long time, then very carefully moved so the box was no longer digging into her back. Hours later after a long stretch of hearing nothing, she got up slowly from her cramped position and slid the closet door open a crack. Dawn was just beginning and she could make out the outlines of the den furniture. Hearing nothing, she crept to the den door, listened, and then slowly opened it. She soon checked each room and knew that no one was inside the house. She took her first deep breath since she awoke in the recliner. She hurried to try the door and was relieved to find it still locked. After a quick check she was satisfied that nothing was missing. The pain in her back was still bothering her and she gratefully fell onto the recliner.

She had been warned over and over about not going out at night unless with others, always carrying her pocketbook in front of her and trying to walk with crowds. She knew about all of the scams tried on the elderly in every city and vowed never to be a victim, but had always felt completely safe in her own home. She did feel safe in the daylight hours. Suddenly she thought, Thank goodness Betsy wasn't with me last night. At least I've got that to be thankful for. She had been dreading having Kendra and Betsy so far away. Now she could only give thanks that they were away and didn't have to know what had happened. When the pain in her back had eased enough she dozed in the recliner. She awoke a couple of hours later, got dressed, retrieved her paper outside the door, and was having coffee when her doorbell rang.

It was Blanche, her next-door neighbor. Before Millie had a chance to say anything, her neighbor asked, "Did you get the morning news?"

"I haven't read much of it. Why? What happened?"

"The police caught two teenagers who had apparently been drinking at a party, and on their way home tried to break into several homes right in our area. They didn't succeed but the police got out a report of them and found and arrested them. It might not be called breaking in as they said they were trying doors to see if they were locked. Thank God they didn't try my door, nor apparently yours either. They really scared some people and the police got a lot of calls. They didn't think the boys even realized that they were frightening people. I hope they punish them enough so they will know that drinking is not a good idea, especially when they are under age and it's against the law. They and their parents are really in trouble.

It took Millie a few moments to grasp what she was telling her, then she was instantly relieved to know what happened and she relaxed completely. What a relief! It was as good as a night's sleep just knowing there was nothing to worry about now.

"Thank you for coming over and telling me about it," said Millie. "Won't you join me for coffee and muffins?"

"Thank you, but no, I really do have to get home. I was just getting back from my walk and decided to stop in and tell you in case you hadn't heard." She started to leave, and then turned and said, "Oh, did you hear about the latest scam on us seniors?" When Millie shook her head, she said, "Someone calls you asking you to help with a survey by answering a few questions about, I believe they said, household appliances. I didn't get the details but the news media tells us not to give out any information and to tell them you are too busy and hang up immediately as it may be a scam. I didn't hear anything more, but they must think we seniors are all naive." She turned to the door again, and then called, "Going to the market in about an hour or so. Anything you need or would you like to go?"

Millie managed to thank her and tell her no, and was glad when she had left. She was holding onto the back of a chair and starting to feel shaky and didn't want Blanche to notice. She had been completely relaxed after she realized that the boys who tried to open her door last night had been apprehended and it was an isolated incident. But when she was told about this latest survey scam a horrible feeling had come over her and she had felt as though she might fall. She had grabbed the back of a chair. Now she carefully moved to sink into it, put her head back and tried to calm down as her heart raced.

In her mind she went over and over the conversation on that day her bid whist friends were coming and that call from the survey lady. She now realized that during the conversation she had inadvertently told a complete stranger that she was an elderly widow living alone. What was she thinking? She had even named all of the appliances in her home. She surely knew better than that. She remembered parts of the conversation. What make of this or that did she own? A survey of popular appliances, she had named the brand of her refrigerator, washer, and smaller items as well. She had been asked if she and her husband were retired. She remembered that she had stupidly told her he had died. Now why did she do that? Why didn't she just tell her that yes, they were retired? When Millie had been asked to help the woman in the survey she had almost said no, but she had felt sorry for the woman. She had sounded so young and that nice soft voice had fooled her.

All of the self-confidence she had slowly gained after Kevin's death was now completely gone and it left her feeling helpless, insecure, and very frightened and vulnerable. One of the warnings they had always given seniors, she realized, was never to give out information to strangers, especially over the phone, as you wouldn't even be able to describe them later. Why hadn't she remembered that? The lady had seemed so nice, but of course she would, and that soft, kind voice, almost like.... Suddenly she gasped in shock. She remembered when Kendra was describing Miss Branish that she had mentioned her very soft voice, and compared it to Miss Heally, Kendra's lower grade teacher's voice. That lady's voice had sounded exactly like that. Was that why Miss Branish wanted to be alone? Could that be it? Was that what she was doing? Someone could be paying that woman to interview unsuspecting homeowners with the request of helping in a survey. Then they would know where elderly people were living alone. Will I have to move, she wondered? Was Miss Branish reporting her calls to Andy? She could have been giving him the list that day we saw them. Neither she nor Kate would have been able to see what they were doing. Maybe he was hiring someone to break into the homes of those on the list, or doing it himself? She knew she should warn Kendra some way as soon as she came home. She would have to tell her daughter the truth about following Miss Branish when she met Andy. She must be told that they know each other. The only other way that could happen would be if she, or one of her "bid whist" friends should be successful in finding them together.

Millie got out the telephone directory to find out if Miss Branish had a telephone, which she would need if her business were the Survey Scam. Then she realized if Miss Branish did have a phone it couldn't have been installed in time to be in this book. She then tried information and found that a C. Branish at that address did indeed have a phone, but it was unlisted. That was something else that Kendra hadn't told her. Millie had not known a phone had been put in that little rented room. Then she suddenly wondered if Kendra even knew it herself. Could Miss Branish have called the phone company and let them in when Kendra was at work? The bills for that phone would be with the tenant's mail going into her own box and Kendra wouldn't see them. Was that possible? By having it unlisted no one could find out her number so she wouldn't be getting calls for anyone to hear the ring. She could make her own calls when she was alone in the house. Unlisted meant another dead end. Then she remembered that the operator had said "C. Branish", so she knew the first name started with a "C". Carol, Carrie, Charlotte, Christine, Catherine, Clara, Connie--the names were endless, and what difference did it make anyway? It was of course possible that she was the sister of Joey Branish, but Clara was just one of many names beginning with "C". Even if she had found out the number and could phone her, she probably wouldn't have got up the courage to do it. She would surely like to hear that voice again. Yes, she felt it could very well be the one she had heard before, that nice soft and sort of whispering voice like Miss Heally's.

That whole privacy thing of Miss Branish--ignoring and avoiding people even those in the same house, fitted right into that little set-up. No wonder she didn't want to talk with anyone. Someone might recognize the voice of a person who had called about a survey. That night Millie turned on the television but didn't hear much of it as she was trying to listen for any strange noises from the outside. Suddenly she heard a few words on the television and her whole attention was on that. The newscaster was reporting the very scam that Blanche had mentioned that morning. Millie was spellbound as she listened to the news. "The scammers tell you they want the home owners to help in a survey to find out the most popular brand names of household appliances. What they really want is your address and names of appliances from large to small. Just tell them nothing at all, and hang up. The scammers, so far, have only stolen small items to sell on the street."

Millie couldn't listen, and turned off the television. She had reported all of her small appliances to this person. She had played right into her hands, and she was now near panic. Miss Branish--was she the one who called her--surely not knowing she was Kendra's mother? The name "Houston" would have no connection to Kendra Thurmose--merely another number in the phone book. That nice soft voice! The more she thought about it, the more frightened she got. She wondered if it would look strange if she visited her sisters twice in one year. Maybe while she was gone these people would break in and take her small appliances, and then she would be safe. Oh dear, she didn't want to move, but she certainly couldn't live like this. Someone had tried her door that night. Was it those teens the police had arrested, or was it someone trying to get in to steal her small appliances?

The next morning Pauline called to see if Millie wanted to go for a short walk with her. Millie told her, and others who called, that her knees were bothering her more than usual. Everyone was sympathetic and wanted to help in any way they could. Pauline had been really upset that more couldn't be done to help Millie's arthritis. "Do you realize," she said, "that they are curing mice of all kinds of things while people like you are still waiting for help?"

Millie couldn't help but laugh, and she had surprised herself that she was able to. She did feel guilty at pretending her joints were hurting more than usual. Yes, they did hurt more from spending the night in a recliner, but not much more than usual. There was no sleep for her at night and she had to get some during the day. She was disgusted with herself, and certainly didn't intend to tell anyone that she had fallen for that survey scam.

That night she methodically checked both doors as always, making sure she had locked the front door, and fastened the chain, then the dead-bolt on the back door. She knew that for another night she would sleep very little as she sat in the recliner and kept peeking out the window and listening. She suddenly thought, "why don't I make a bed in the closet?" Wouldn't that be better than the living room recliner and having to rush into the closet if anyone came? She piled the shoes up on one end of the closet, spread out all of the soft blankets she could find, put two big pillows at the end, then a folded sheet and blanket on top of that. She took her cordless phone and flashlight into the closet with her and lay down on the improvised bed. She wasn't sure it was better, but if anyone did get in they would think she wasn't there as her bed was completely made up in the bedroom. She still slept very little as she kept listening for the slightest sound.

In the morning, she didn't feel quite as tired, so she may have slept a little, but she was stiff from the hard floor. Any number of blankets couldn't take the place of a mattress or comfortable chair, and she slowly and painfully got to her feet and into the living room. Again relief flowed through her when she saw the DVD and CD players still there. She had half expected them to be gone in spite of her wakeful vigil and locked doors. Nothing was missing from the kitchen either. Did that mean that no one could get in, or that they hadn't got to her name on the list yet? Suddenly she realized that she would like nothing better than to hand over whatever was wanted to whoever wanted it. "Here, take it. Take what you want and give me back my life." She reached out her door, retrieved her morning paper, and hurried through it finding break-ins and robberies as usual. That was all she was looking for now. She had done just what the other old folks did that they were always mentioning on TV, radio, and in the daily papers. She had wondered why so many people seemed to fall for those scams. Now she had done something just as stupid--and she also knew now that it had been a scam. She should notify the police, but what could they do? They certainly wouldn't send someone to guard her house. Besides, she didn't want them or anyone else to know what she had done, and of course they knew about it. If she could only talk with Kendra and let her know what she suspected of her Miss Branish, but certainly not when she was so far away. What a terrible way to make a living. Of course it might not be true, but it certainly all seems to fit. She could still remember that kind, soft voice and also remembered that she had felt sorry for her having to make a living by taking surveys over the phone.

After her bath that night she got dressed again. She would stay in Kevin's recliner tonight and would be already dressed in the morning instead of wearing her robe half the day while she dozed. She hadn't been very comfortable in the closet and had been much stiffer than usual today. It hadn't helped that much, so she spent another terrifying night peeking through the gap in the drapes. She could see through the haze from the streetlight in front of the next house. She was looking for anyone who approached her door. If she heard or saw anything suspicious she would quickly call the police. She had memorized their number. If she were too frightened to remember it, she would call 911. She now kept her cordless phone near her. Right now she was clutching it and repeating the number of the police department over and over. What a way to live! She was only waiting for daylight so she could get some sleep in the recliner. She did leave the makeshift bed in the closet. If anyone should approach her door she would dash into the closet, and now she kept the cordless with her. She had also left a small flashlight in the closet so she could see enough to make a call.

That survey was always on her mind--and when she saw another article in the paper of a break-in she was really frightened. The woman was thankful that she had been away from home at the time. This only reinforced Millie's own fear. Fear? It was pure terror for Millie. She almost wished they would break in whether she was here or not, and get it over with. Then she supposed they would cross her off their list.

CHAPTER 7

As Millie was finishing reading her paper with half of her mind and wondering with the other half what she should do, she had decided she would have to move. How could she ever explain to Kendra why she would like to move? Maybe she should tell...No, she realized that she didn't want Kendra to know she had been taken in by this scam. She would think her mother was not able to live alone. Millie had been trying to get her and Betsy to move in with her. She certainly didn't want to feel as though she had to be taken care of. She rested a while longer in the recliner, but as exhausted as she was, she couldn't seem to relax enough to get much rest. She knew she had to think of a solution before Kendra and Betsy came home from camp. Moving was the only solution she could come up with and..... Suddenly it came to her like a comic strip light bulb over her head--A security system of course! Why in the world hadn't she thought of that in the first place? If she got that, she would be able to stay right here in her own home and be safe. Wide awake now she got up as fast as she could, grabbed the Telephone Directory and scanned the yellow pages.

After a few more sleepless nights, she had a sophisticated, expensive, security system installed. It had the one touch police and fire emergency button, and chime alert if a door or window was left open. If anyone walked near the area around her house a floodlight would go on, and a camera would activate. If anyone were ignorant enough after that to move a window or door even the slightest or cut the telephone wire, a siren would go off. That siren would scare anyone away and notify the police as well as her neighbors. And best of all there was a prominent sign on the lawn advertising the system, and that alone should deter almost anyone from going farther. If they didn't believe that sign, they would believe it when that bright light went on, or the next step with that alarm. The people who installed it explained to her that she could have a system where the alarm would not go off here, but would go off at the police station and they could be there in minutes. She opted for the one that instantly activated the alarm. Of course she would like to have the intruder caught but what if the police were delayed? No, she wanted the loud alarm. In fact she ordered anything and everything that would keep her safe and give her back her peace of mind. She hoped an arrest could still be made. She knew the security system had been installed, thoroughly tested, and she had been checked out in using it. Millie crawled into her own bed and slept soundly. She awoke refreshed for the first time since that first horrible night in the closet when someone was trying her door. She didn't think that it had been those mixed-up kids from the party. She thought it was more likely someone from that survey scam. But at last she could put that lapse-of-sense telephone conversation of the survey out of her mind. The next morning she told Pauline that her hip was much better. She tucked the directions for the alarm into her jewelry box for safe keeping in case she needed to check it, and put the whole experience out of her mind.

The following morning Millie got a call from Kendra. After talking about how they were and what each of them were doing, Kendra asked, "Mother, you do have a key to my house don't you?"

"Yes, it's in my jewelry box. Did you want something?"

"I hate to bother you, Mom, and it was careless of me to leave it, but I would like a list of names and addresses that I left on the small desk by the kitchen door. I won't need it for a while--in fact not until near the last of next week, so wait for a nice day when you have nothing planned and call Handy Harry's won't you?"

"Sure, glad to. I'll send it out as soon as I get it." They talked a little longer and verified the address of the camp where they were staying. Her mother assured Kendra that she was doing fine, but of course missed her daughter and granddaughter. She put the phone down and copied the address onto a business size envelope, stamped it, and put it in her pocketbook until she could go to the cottage. The timing couldn't have been better--after the first good sleep in almost a week. By afternoon of the same day however, Millie began to realize just how much she had charged to her credit card in buying that expensive security system.

That night, instead of again sleeping peacefully, she was wide-awake most of the night thinking about the large amount she had charged to her credit card with that high interest rate. She knew the interest rate had gone way up, but she always paid it up at the end of the month so it didn't matter. She had thought of nothing else all afternoon. The only thing she had been thinking of when she ordered the system was getting some sleep--just getting into her bed and sleeping. Now she turned on the light and reached for her calculator and again went over her income and expenses. There was no way it could stretch to pay off that extra debt. She just could not do it. Why hadn't she thought of this? With that large interest rate she would be a long time paying it off. In fact she would do well to just manage the interest. What could she do now? She was no longer worried about a break-in, but she was definitely worried about that large debt. She had assured Kendra that she would be fine while they were away. Now look at the mess she was in. Well she had been managing nicely before this. Her income had always been adequate, but it didn't allow for this large an expense. She had known she could manage the quarterly amounts for the monitoring of it, but hadn't even thought about how she could pay for the purchasing price on her credit card as well. That combined payment was way over the top of her budget. She knew now that she shouldn't have included so many extras. She was just so tired she wasn't thinking clearly.

After a few more sleepless nights, she thought of a solution and that morning she called the local newspaper to advertise her piano for sale. It was a lovely piano, but she kept telling herself she really didn't play it as much as she used to, and Betsy seemed to show no interest in learning to play it--she only wanted to learn to read. Millie had thought about it a long time and knew there was no other solution. She had nothing else that would begin to cover the cost of this expensive security system. Her library of books would take too long, and probably wouldn't be enough anyway. Besides she knew Betsy would want those some day. Later when a woman called about her ad for the piano, she described it to her, and then gave her the address. Almost immediately she felt scared. She had given a stranger her address. She had turned into a nervous wreck, and was thinking, what if a robber came instead after asking a friendly-sounding woman accomplice to make the call for him? Maybe this was another scam where they were watching for ads like hers as a way to get in to see what else she had.

Pauline called soon after to ask her if she felt like taking a walk with her. Millie told her she felt like it, but had to be there when the buyers came to look at her piano, and asked her to come over for coffee and maybe they could take a short walk later. She didn't want to be alone when the people came either, and that would be nice.

While they were enjoying their popovers and coffee Pauline asked, "Why did you decide to sell that piano?"

"I haven't played it much lately and can put that space to better use with more book cases," she said. "You know books are my passion, also Betsy shares my love for books and reading. She would be much happier to have my collection of books than that piano. That's an awfully large piece of furniture to move around with you, and expensive to move."

Almost exactly the time they had agreed on, the woman arrived with her husband and two neighbors, one who had a truck. They seemed happy with the piano but made her an offer lower than she was asking, and she didn't dare refuse it. Maybe she could have got her asking price if she had insisted. She knew it was worth much more but didn't want to miss this sale. She was thinking of going through the scare of giving her address to another stranger. They paid her, then the husband and neighbors, who came equipped with a ramp and dolly, muscled it into the truck and wrapped and tied blankets around the beautiful piano. Millie watched with mixed emotions.

After they had left, the two neighbors went for their slow walk around the block. Millie knew that Pauline, who was younger and thinner, would have walked much faster if she had been alone but she seemed to want Millie to accompany her, as she kept asking her. Her friend knew that Millie was supposed to exercise a little each day, and she wanted to help her.

Now Pauline asked, "Why did you let them have that piano at a lower price than you were asking? It was surely worth much more."

"I didn't want to give my address over the phone to another stranger. I guess it was silly but, living alone, I don't like the idea of giving it to just anyone who happens to answer an add."

"I can understand that, but they came prepared to buy it. They had all of the equipment needed, and even brought a couple of neighbors to help load it. They would have paid the asking price if you had stuck with it."

"Yes, I guess they would have." Millie sighed, and then said, "Anyway, I'm glad it's sold, and I can forget it."

Her neighbor said, "You have the security system now, so why are you so worried about giving your address? You are certainly protected now."

"You're right of course. I am protected," and she suddenly felt confident. Whatever was lost she had no reason to worry now.

"You gave a lot of lessons on that piano, didn't you?"

"Yes, and I enjoyed that. It was great when I found a child who really took naturally to it and wanted to learn. Usually they came only because their mothers wanted them to learn to play, and weren't very enthusiastic about practicing."

Even while visiting, Millie's mind kept jumping to the amount she had received for her piano. It wouldn't be enough to cover the credit card debt but if she was very careful she should be able to pay off the balance before the end of the year, or maybe a few months beyond. That would mean...well, it couldn't be helped. She would just have to pay that horrendous interest for a few months more.

When they got back from their walk Pauline asked Millie to come in to see her new afghan that her daughter-in-law had made for her. It was beautiful and had a design of Michael's restaurant in the center.

"Did she make that pattern herself?" asked Millie, impressed with the handiwork.

"It took her a while to work it out," said Pauline, but she is quite an artist and loves doing it. Then she showed Millie some of the paintings. As she was viewing a painting of "The Palace", Millie asked, "Is the addition to Michael's restaurant finished yet?"

"Oh yes, about a week ago. He had decided on a room that could be converted to a screened porch in the summer," and she pointed to the side where this new addition had been added. Then she asked, "Has Kendra's tenant returned yet? I haven't seen her in the restaurant for a while. I was also wondering when Kendra and Betsy were returning from camp?"

While they were seated in the den admiring the paintings, Millie answered, "They are due back at the end of the week. At least Kendra and Betsy are. As far as I know Miss Branish is still there."

"Really? I was at Michael's house for dinner last Thursday and Corrie mentioned that your daughter and granddaughter were on a camping trip and she also said there had been no lights over there for a couple of weeks."

"Well then she must be visiting somewhere too," said Millie, but she wondered what was going on. Had that woman moved out? If so, did Kendra know she was gone?

When Millie returned to her house a little later, she sat looking at the spot where her beloved piano had been, knowing how much she would miss it. After resting a short while she vacuumed where it had been, then moved two light chairs and an end table into the space, and an ornamental vase onto the table. She sat in her recliner, exhausted after the exercise, and leaned back wondering again where Miss Branish was and if Kendra knew she was gone.

After many more calls from people who wanted to buy her piano, Millie knew for sure she didn't get anywhere near what she should have for that beautiful piece of furniture. Pauline was right. They had definitely come intending to buy it, so why did she let them pay less than asked? But she refused to dwell on that, and was thankful that she could now tell anyone who called that it had been sold.

Their next Bid-Whist meeting was at Mable's this time and she quickly called each of them to inform them they would have their get-together at her grandson's summer cottage unless it rained, then it would be at her house as usual. They all loved meeting at the cottage where they could have their games and refreshments on the porch overlooking lake St. Shelter. Not only that, but Mable's grandson always picked each of them up and took them to his cottage and returned them later to their homes. They were also informed that refreshments would be supplied as usual. None of the four friends had to do anything but enjoy the day. Millie decided she would forget everything that had been worrying her and just have a carefree day.

When Mable's grandson, Kerby, came to pick up Millie and Kate, he was driving his convertible with the top down. "It's up to you ladies," he said. "If you prefer, say the word and I'll put the top up."

"Let's keep it down until we get to Belle's," suggested Kate. "If anyone would want it up she would be the one. Let's let her decide," thinking to herself that she would anyway.

"Good idea," said Millie.

"You two can get in front with me--plenty of room, and the others can ride in the back," and Kerby held the door for them.

They picked up his grandmother Mable first, and she was delighted with the fresh-air ride, but when Belle came out of her house a little later, they could tell by the look on her face and her immaculate hair-do that the top would go up. After Kerby had opened the door for her and got her seated in back with his grandmother, he asked Belle, "Top up or down?"

"Up, please," she replied, and he pushed the button to raise the top. Mable couldn't hold back her giggle. It was a nice drive and they were delighted when they arrived at the lake, which was clear and blue and not a ripple on it--a perfect summer day.

Kerby and his wife Holly had got everything ready for them. They had the table set up for their games, and refreshments in the refrigerator with plates, napkins, and cups on the counter, and coffee maker ready to turn on and water to heat for tea. They visited briefly with the ladies, then left for the afternoon, telling them the cottage was theirs, and they would be back about 5:00 p.m. They also checked to make sure that Mable had their cell phone number with her.

After they had left, Belle said, "All right, this is my report. Rita, the young teacher I know, has gone over to Craig Heights. I hadn't known she was a substitute teacher. Her grandmother told me she was at the Rainbow and I assumed she was permanent. I'll get over to Craig Heights as soon as I can and find out. I'm sure if Andy was new when she was at the Rainbow School that she would know where he came from."

"Why didn't you call me?" asked Mable. I told you I'd take you to wherever the woman came from and I'd be glad to take you to see your young teacher friend too."

"I didn't know for sure until last evening or I would have called, and I wasn't sure you'd want to drive over there either, as it's so congested."

"Unless you are afraid to ride with me, I'd be glad to."

"Okay, name the time and we'll take care of it."

"How about tomorrow morning at 9:00 a.m.?"

"Fine, I'll be ready. Thanks Mable. Don't worry, Millie, we'll find out something soon and will call you as soon as I can."

"Oh, thank you both. That would help so much if we could find that missing link."

"I wish we could have gone sooner," said Mable to Belle, "and we could have had news today."

"This is the end of their spring vacation so we couldn't have gone earlier. Remember, I just found out last evening." They soon got to the important business of playing, all thrilled that they might have an answer soon.

"Now," asked Millie, "how do we start--Kate and I are partners this time aren't we?" They were soon involved in their game.

In the middle of the first hand a man and woman came to the door and asked if Kerby or Holly were here. Mable told them her grandson and wife wouldn't be back until 5:00 p.m. The man told her that some of the cottages had been broken into and they wondered if the Tromba's cottage had been one of them.

"They didn't mention anything about a break-in," said Mable. "When did it happen?"

"We think yesterday afternoon or evening," said the man, "People are just beginning to notice it. It looks as though they either opened a window or door by prying so it wasn't noticeable immediately."

"Not until they missed something," said the woman. "We're the Crandall's--third cottage down. "Would you please tell them when they return what has happened? But if they were here this morning they probably would have noticed anything amiss before they left. It looks as though they only broke into places where no car was parked. They probably came in by boat and no one would have thought anything of seeing another boat around."

After the Crandall's had gone Mable decided she wouldn't call Kerby and Holly and ruin their afternoon. She checked the windows and doors for prying damage and found nothing wrong. "They couldn't do anything more if they were here," said Mable, "and they can check when they get back." The four friends finished their game.

They moved their chairs so they could all look out over the lake then brought the prepared refreshments out to the porch table.

"I could get used to this," said Millie, as she gazed out over the lake with the boats and skiers.

"It would be lovely until dark," said Kate, "then I'd feel awfully alone."

Since each of them lived alone they all agreed and their conversation again turned to the crime today and how different it used to be when they were young, and what could be done now to stop it. Mable said, "I hate to tell Kerby and Holly that they are having more break-ins. I suppose other kids are growing up to the age of getting into trouble. Do they have to go through that stage?"

"I'm sure most of them don't," said Millie. "It all depends on how they are brought up. I think most kids are basically good," and the others agreed with her.

"I thought surely I'd have something to report at this meeting," said Belle. "I was so disappointed that I couldn't speak to Rita. Did any of you hear anyone trying your door when those teenagers were roaming the streets?" No one had, and Belle continued, "One of my neighbors heard someone trying the door and called the police. That may have helped the police to find and arrest them. I do feel sorry for their parents though."

"So much crime," said Millie. I'm grateful for all of you for what you have done for me."

I wished I could call Rita," said Belle, "but no one seemed to know her address. All I can do is go to the school. As soon as we find out anything we'll let you know MIllie."

"Tomorrow morning is wonderful," said Millie. None of us has found anyone who has heard of her. We have all checked everywhere and everyone we could think of, and no one could remember hearing the name except in relation to Joey Branish, or they had heard there was a Miss Branish renting from Kendra Thurmose. I Hope finding something about Andy will help us find out about Miss Branish." She took a big breath and let it out slowly. "I was wishing Kendra had got references, but maybe we will find out better by just questioning people who knew her and not someone she picked out to furnish her with a reference. Everyone has someone who would give a good reference, maybe for a price."

"But Millie, we don't know that Miss Branish came from the same place Andy did. We just hope to find out where he came from."

"I know. I'm just hoping real hard, and I'd be happy to get some information about him too even if it doesn't lead to her."

They spent the rest of the time relaxing and visiting while watching the fantastic view of the lake and mountains.

Kerby and Holly returned shortly after 5:00 p.m. to visit with Grammy Mable and her friends for a while before escorting the ladies home. They also found no signs of a break-in and mentioned that their car had been parked right by the side porch. They were hoping that this was an isolated case and that there would be no more break-ins.

The next morning was sunny and beautiful and Kate and Millie decided to go to Kendra's house and get the list she wanted. Kate told her she would be over in about twenty minutes, so Millie waited for her before calling the cab. She was glad Kate was free to go with her as she didn't want to be in that house alone with a criminal, and she felt quite sure by now that Miss Branish was a criminal. Even if she had been gone, as Pauline had thought, Millie felt she could easily be back by now.

When Millie and Kate walked into Kendra's house it seemed so quiet that she thought if Miss Branish was still living there that she must be out. Kate reminded Millie that the tenant might be home and keeping quiet. She wouldn't know who had come in, and maybe Millie should knock on her door just to let her know whom she was and why she was here. After all if the woman was here and thought she was alone in the house she could be frightened.

Millie agreed it was a good idea. She might hear that voice, as she had been wanting to. She had retrieved the list Kendra wanted and put it in the envelope for mailing, and then Kate waited at the foot of the stairs as Millie went up and knocked on the door of the little rented room. She knocked again louder, and called out her name and told her she was Kendra's mother, and then came back down disappointed that she hadn't heard her speak. Michael's family was probably right in thinking that Miss Branish was gone as well as Kendra and Betsy. Kendra hadn't mentioned it to her mother, but she apparently hadn't been concerned about her mother's visit frightening her tenant either. She must have known her tenant was gone and just not thought to mention it.

When they got outside Kate said, "It was awfully dark in there."

"I thought so too," said Millie. "She must be gone and the drapes were closed." She mailed the list that Kendra had wanted, and tried to forget about the incident. After all she had been concerned that Miss Branish was alone in Kendra's house. Now she could put that worry to rest. She probably wasn't even there, but how she wished she could have heard her voice. She felt sure hers was the voice she had heard when she answered the survey call.

That evening a very tired Belle called Millie and told her they had to hunt for Rita, as she wasn't at the school that day but Mable said she didn't mind and we found her. Rita remembered that Andrew Miller came from the Hanover District and we will get over there in the morning. We were too tired today."

"Oh thank you Belle and I'll call Mable too but you have done enough. Kate and I can get over there easily and."

"I'm sure Mable won't want you to. She was delighted that she could do something to help you. She had tried so hard to find Kendra's tenant and Andy together, but is looking forward to going over there and investigating."

"Whether you find anything or not, Belle, I'll be just as grateful for you trying so hard," said Millie. "I'll call Mable right off and will, at least, mention that we can go easily."

"Kendra and Betsy will be coming home soon," said Belle, "and you will be anxious to see them. You can call Mable and try and convince her, but I don't think so. She's little, but Oh My!" They were both laughing when they said goodbye."

Millie called Mable immediately, but Mable said, "no way". She and Belle were going over in the morning and would report as soon as possible.

The next night Mable called all excited, "We found a lot of people in the Hanover School District and in the neighborhood who praised Andy Miller as a wonderful person, but not one of them had ever heard of the name Branish. I'm sorry but she couldn't have come from that district. Many people seemed upset that Andy had left their town so quickly, and we got the impression he didn't say goodbye to anyone. They still had nothing but praise for him."

"Thank you, Mable. You both must be exhausted. I'm so grateful and you have worked so hard for me. At least I can feel good about Kendra's friend now. He must have his reasons for leaving the Hanover District, as well as not going to Kendra's house," but she was thinking and hoped they were good and legitimate reasons."

"I hoped it would make you feel better."

"Oh it does. I think Kendra really cares for him and I didn't want to see her hurt. Thanks for bringing me this news."

After they were through visiting Millie called Belle to thank her as well, then Kate, so everyone was up to date. She was still worried about

Kendra's tenant, and told her friends it probably was not necessary to investigate her any more since Andy had seemed so happy to see her in the restaurant that day. She wasn't sure about her yet, but sincerely hoped she would be no more of a criminal than Andy was. She sat in her recliner and reached for her notebook. This time she would add a happier message.

CHAPTER 8

By the time Kendra and Betsy returned tanned and happy from their camping trip, things were back to normal for Millie except for that high-interest debt she was slowly paying off.

"Grammy, it was super. I'm going again next year aren't I Mom?"

"We'll see, we'll see. Let's recover from this one first," she laughed. Then to her mother, "It wasn't as tiring as I thought it would be. In fact it went pretty well. It was a new experience for both Betsy and me." Then to Betsy, she asked, "Are you going to give Grammy her gift?"

"Oh, I forgot," and she spun around to get it from her mother's tote bag. "I hope you like it, Grammy," she said as she handed the brightly wrapped gift to her grandmother.

It was a tee shirt with the words, "Best Grammy in the World".

"I love it, Honey. What a nice thing to do. It's the right size too. Thank you," and she held it up and looked at it again.

"Mommy didn't know if you'd wear it, but I knew you would."

"You bet I will." She looked up to see Kendra hiding a smile. When Betsy went to the toy box Kendra laughed and said quietly, "I seem to remember your saying once, 'If you have something to say, either say it or write it, but don't wear it.' You also said you didn't want strangers staring at your bosom to see what you had to say."

Her mother smiled and said, "I hadn't seen my granddaughter's message then."

Kendra asked, "How did things go for you while we were gone? You never gave me much detail over the phone."

"Well, I knew it was long distance and anyway I wanted to hear your news. Everything is fine here. You know I don't have a very varied schedule. I was busy with my friends and you also know how I love to read."

"I saw your security sign the first thing. That's a great idea, Mom. Why didn't we think of it before, knowing how concerned you have been about crime? I've heard they are very expensive though. Why don't I help you out with the..."

"Oh, no. I'm fine. Senior citizens get a lot of discounts when they shop, and you need your money for other things."

"Nothing can be more important than your safety and Betsy's too. She is often with you, so let me help with...."

"No Kendra, really, I heard about the system and decided it would be a good idea and got it. I'm glad I did and it will make us all feel better." She didn't want anything to diminish the feeling of confidence she had gained back. "Maybe you should have one put in too."

"Maybe I should, but I do live quite near the police station and that should surely make it safer."

Kendra and Betsy stayed for lunch with Millie, and then Kendra said they should go home to unpack and pick up their mail at the post office.

"If it would help I'd be glad to have Betsy stay with me while you unpack and do your errands," her mother told her.

"If you are sure you really feel like it, it would help a lot."

After Kendra had left, Betsy talked excitedly, her words tumbling over each other, trying to tell her grandmother everything they did during the camping trip. She was telling her about their buddy system and the boat rides, then suddenly interrupted herself, "I learned a little bit to swim. When I sink I learned to stop breathing until I get my head back out."

"Well I should think that would be a big help," said her grandmother between bursts of laughter, "and when you learn not to sink and how to move along, you'll really be swimming. I missed you a lot," she added as she reached to pick her up. She realized she couldn't lift her. "You've grown since I picked you up I think."

"We all grew while we were there--Mommy too."

"Was she happy about that?"

"I don't think so, but I was. She wouldn't eat dessert any more, so I had to eat hers. If you want to sit down Grammy, you can sit, then I can climb up if you can't lift me any more."

"Let's try that. We'll sit in your Grandpa's recliner," and she sat down. Betsy ran to get a book and came back and scrambled up into her lap. "Now we can read."

By the end of the afternoon when Kendra arrived to pick up Betsy, Millie was tired and ready for a quiet evening. Kendra sat down for a few minutes before rushing off with Betsy. "You look tired, Mom," she said. "I'm afraid Betsy is too much for you."

"Oh no, she isn't. She spruces me up and makes me feel better-- honest. I am tired now, but it's a nice tired."

"I know you love her, Mom, but it won't help anyone if you get sick."

"I know, and when I'm tired I just tell Betsy that her Grammy is a little tired, and she's willing to play quietly. She is really so good about it."

"Thanks for all of your help, Mom," then she called to Betsy, "What are you doing? Mommy's ready to go."

Betsy came out of the den with an armful of books. "Grammy said I could take them home to read. Did you know I could read?"

"You can't read those, can you?"

"I can read the front words, can't I Grammy?"

"Well, yes I guess you could say that. You know the names of all of them don't you?"

"Yup, I do--and I told Grammy that I ate your dessert at camp, Mom."

Her mother laughed as she got up and took the books from Betsy to put in her tote. "Yes, I'll have to find a diet and stick with it," she said to her mother. "I have seven pounds to lose."

"Those diets are hogwash," said her mother. "Just try to eat healthy and only have an occasional dessert. Even if you are dieting you have to stay healthy and enjoy what you eat. In one magazine I found two diets and one of them said if you just put a handful of raisins on your cereal in the morning, there you are--that makes one of those healthy fruit servings. The other diet mentioned that if you leave out the raisins on your cereal you are saving about 100 calories right there. It's all in the way you look at it. Can you imagine putting those two diets in the same magazine?"

Both women laughed, and Kendra said, "You're right, Mom. I'll just try to eat healthy and cut down a little and choose better. Come on, Betsy. Time to go. Give Grammy a kiss, and we're off."

It was about a week later when Kendra, Betsy, and Millie went into her living room that Kendra suddenly exclaimed, "Mother--your piano. Where is it?"

"I hid it," said her mother mischievously. Kendra laughed, and Betsy looked at her wide-eyed, then all around the room, which made her mother and grandmother laugh more. Then Millie said, "Seriously, I decided to get rid of it. It took up so much room and I hardly ever played it. Someone was looking for one and I realized I might just as well sell it and have more room for my books. You didn't want it, did you?" she asked.

"Heavens, no. I don't have enough time for all of my projects as it is, but I did think you enjoyed it. You used to play it a lot."

"Well, I used to do a lot of things that I no longer do. It just seemed like it took up a lot of room for what little I used it. I played it a lot more when your Dad was here. He liked to hear me play some of our old favorites in the evenings after dinner."

Kendra didn't mention it again and just assumed that it had made her mother too sad thinking of her Dad. She did remember her playing it more when he was alive.

The next Bid-Whist afternoon at Kate's house Belle mentioned a play she had attended with her neighbor. It had been put on by the Rainbow School. "Those kids are really good," she said. "I hear they have a great new Acting Instructor who joined the faculty quite recently and has a knack for keeping them interested and doing well. The kids seem to like him and try harder to make everything work."

When Millie heard that, she suddenly realized that she hadn't seen, or heard anything about, Andy since Mable and Belle had received the great report from his hometown. Kendra hadn't mentioned him since they had returned from their camping trip. He must be the one Belle was referring to--the new acting instructor.

"He used to be an actor himself," said Mable. "and they say he was very good."

"And quite a ladies' man I hear," said Belle.

Kate and Millie exchanged quick glances, and then suddenly Millie said, "I think that new instructor, ex-actor, that you mentioned is Andy, the young man Kendra is dating, and you investigated. I just realized whom you were talking about. I was so sure he had an ulterior motive for seeking out Kendra, and I was very wrong according to your investigation. But I don't want to think of Kendra being hurt either."

"I'm sorry, Millie," said Belle. I never connected him with that young man at all. You know people can say anything, and I shouldn't be so quick to repeat things either. I didn't mean to say anything that would hurt or worry you."

"I know that, Belle. It's all right and it's always better to know."

"I wonder too if anyone has heard anything new about the survey scam," asked Kate.

"I heard of a woman," said Mable, "who is thinking of moving away because she was interviewed and, not thinking, gave out all of the information they asked for. She is frantic now. Millie suddenly felt again that Miss Branish was the one who was behind the survey scam. She felt like calling the police and giving them the name and address of Miss Branish. She could do it anonymously, couldn't she? If she was just a busy writer, she could prove it. And if she was the one who called her about the survey, then they would have at least one of the scammers. It made her furious that so many people could be hurt and frightened by the actions of a small band of dishonest people. She thought of the many times she had wished she could sit down to her piano and play away her frustrations. But of course if she did tell the police it would interrupt Kendra's life too when they arrived at her house. Oh dear why did life have to get so complicated? She wanted Betsy to continue at "Toddler Town," but didn't want it paid for by a criminal. What should she do? Of course she didn't have proof either that the woman was doing anything underhanded. Millie hadn't got up her courage to tell Kendra what she suspected of Miss Branish. She also knew Kendra--and that imagination hang-up of hers concerning her mother would surely surface again. So what good would it do if she wouldn't be taken seriously? I'm glad people that know Andy like him but she thought would they know of something like...? No, I can't think like that. She was worried about the fact that she hadn't seen Andy around. She wasn't very talkative the rest of the visit and her friends knew just how she felt and what she was thinking. No one wants to think his or her daughter cares for someone who may not be true to her. Could those people who praised him so highly know about something that personal? And even if Andy did prove to be as ethical as his friends thought of him, couldn't he have been taken in by this Miss Branish, whatever she was to him?

After refreshments, and when Belle and Mable had left, Millie stayed a few minutes to help Kate with the cleanup.

She wanted to tell Kate about the Survey Scam but her self confidence was so shattered now and her shame too fresh. That was all anyone was talking about so it was fresh on everyone's minds.

"You are really concerned with the relationship of Kendra and her friend Andy aren't you?" asked Kate.

"Yes, I am, about their personal relationship, but what bothers me more is Kendra's tenant, and of course what connection there is between Andy and her. I don't know anything much about her, and she's living with Kendra and Betsy. At least I assume she is now, but she seemed to have been gone during the time they were camping."

"I wonder if she really was gone or just didn't answer you when we were at Kendra's house that day. But If you're really concerned," said Kate, "and I can understand why you don't want to make things harder for Kendra, maybe we could do some different kind of detective work." Then she laughed and added, "I remember when you were determined to become a private detective, but don't remember when you changed your mind about your career."

"I'm sure it was when I first sat down to a piano."

"And now you have sold it. How could you?"

"Easily. I'm an old woman now, my husband is gone, and I have other interests."

"Then you're free to go back to your first love of detective work. So how about if we do something about it?"

"Like what?" asked Millie, "spending our free days following Kendra's tenant around some more? No thank you."

"No, not exactly, I know Mable and Belle are still trying to follow her, or at least go where she might be and hope to see them together, but we could try something else. Why not have lunch once in a while at the Purple.... No, how about the Waterfall Restaurant? That's even better. If we could be seated on the porch we would have a good view of anyone near the Longman's game room. You never know, and apparently she goes there often. How about it?"

"I suppose we could try it," but she was thinking that whatever shady game the lady might be playing it had nothing to do with Longman's. She felt so sure that it had been that lady's voice on the phone of the survey scam--but going to lunch with Kate would be a pleasant pastime anyway.

"Any better idea?" asked Kate.

"No, let's try it. I'm having Betsy tomorrow, but how about next Tuesday? Are you free for lunch then?" she asked.

"I am, but could we make it next Wednesday instead? I'm pretty sure that Mable said it was on a Wednesday about noon when she saw the lady watching the children."

"Was it on a Wednesday too that you saw Miss Branish there?"

"I don't remember which day, but it was in the early evening that I saw her, and I'm sure Mable saw the lady on a Wednesday about noon. At least it sounded as though it could be her. In the meantime if either of us thinks of anything else to try, or hears of anything else, we'll jot it down. We can't very well have a detective following her around, and we couldn't do that very long ourselves without being conspicuous, but we might find out something. Maybe we can figure out what she is doing there."

Millie was thinking that Mable, Kate, and Belle all thought Miss Branish was doing something underhanded, but had no idea that it was the survey scam that she was probably guilty of. Secrets, secrets, she hated them but she couldn't let anyone know of the dumb thing she had done. Falling right into that survey scam was so frightening and embarrassing that she would keep that one to herself. She couldn't believe she had been gullible enough to fall for that. If she confided in Kate, she would feel even more vulnerable just knowing that someone else knew about it. She would prefer that to be her own little secret. She wished sometimes they hadn't followed Miss Branish, but if they hadn't she wouldn't have known that the lady and Andy knew each other. But how important was that if she never told Kendra? She now was quite sure that Andy was not an accomplice of any kind--didn't she? She seemed to vacillate on this one. Would the people where he came from know about it if he was?

The next time Kendra brought Betsy over to stay with her grandmother for a few hours, Millie mentioned to her daughter that she hadn't seen Andy around and wondered if he was all right.

"Oh yes, he's fine. He has been visiting his family for a while."

"Oh, I thought Belle said the new Acting teacher helped the students put on a new show. I guess I just assumed he was the one."

"It probably was. He came back long enough to put on a play at the Summer School. He's going back now that the play is over." She didn't mention whether she had seen him lately and Millie wondered again what was going on, but said no more about him.

After Kendra left, Millie asked Betsy if Miss Branish still went out at night.

"I don't see her any more," she said.

"She's still living there isn't she?"

"I don't think so. I don't see her."

"How strange," thought Millie. She was wondering if Andy Miller and Miss Branish might both be away. Had Miss Branish moved her operation to some other place? Could Andy possibly have been talked into.... No, all of his friends couldn't be wrong. Why hadn't Kendra mentioned that Miss Branish was away too? She wondered if she planned to come back, if she was still paying rent, and if her belongings were still at Kendra's. Then she asked Betsy, "Have you seen Patty since you got back?"

"No, but she and Andy came to see us at camp."

"Did they stay there?"

"No, we went to a restaurant, then they took Mommy and me back to camp because we had Story and Rest Time, and Andy and Patty went to visit someone."

Later Kendra had stopped in to her mother's for a while, and then mentioned that she had some errands and they had better get started.

"Then why doesn't Betsy stay right here with me?" asked her mother, "and you can get your errands done and get some rest and Betsy can go to bed here."

"No Mother," said Kendra, "You looked so much more rested when we first got back and I don't want you to have any extra responsibilities."

"But I'm not tired in the least, and I really love having her with me, so why not?"

"Can I stay, Mommy? Can I please?"

Kendra laughed, and said, "It seems to be unanimous, so if you're sure you feel like it, then I might go out this evening. I don't want you to overdo though."

"Don't worry, we'll be fine. You just go out and enjoy yourself." Millie was curious but didn't ask what her plans for the evening were. She was just thankful that she had shared that much with her. But if Andy was away, was she going out alone or with someone else?

CHAPTER 9

After Betsy was tucked in for the night, Millie decided to take a leisurely bath and skip the news tonight and go straight to bed. She was just getting a towel out of the linen closet when the doorbell rang. She hurried to the door thinking that Kendra had come back, but cautiously turned on the outside light and looked through the peephole. It was a policeman, who immediately held up his badge and asked if he could speak with her a minute. She quickly turned off the security and opened the door; sure that something had happened to Kendra. "Come in. What is it?" she anxiously asked.

"Nothing to be concerned about, Mrs. Houston. I don't usually ring doorbells quite this late unless it's an emergency. I saw your light and I do need some information so decided to try. I shouldn't have assumed you were awake because your light was on, but I'm glad you were. Could you tell me where your daughter, Kendra Thurmose, is tonight?"

"No, what's wrong?" she asked anxiously.

"I don't know that anything is wrong. I just wanted to ask her a few questions. Do you have any idea where she might be?" "No, I don't know. I'm keeping her daughter with me, as she was busy tonight. She doesn't confide in me."

"If you don't mind, maybe you can help me. Can you tell me how many people live in her house?"

"My daughter, my granddaughter, and a lady renter. Why?"

"No one answers the door, and I thought you might know where everyone is."

"I only know my granddaughter is with me. I don't know where my daughter was going, and I know nothing about the renter except that she is a writer."

"Nothing else? Do you know if she goes out much?"

"I have no idea. In fact I've never even met her. I would assume that she would be working on her writing a lot of the time."

"Well, I'm sorry to bother you, Mrs. Houston, and I thank you for your time."

"Why do you want this information if nothing is wrong?"

"Just routine, just routine. Do you live alone here?"

"Yes, I do, except of course when my granddaughter is visiting me, like tonight. Is that important?

"Probably not. We just gather information periodically in the neighborhood. Lots of records to keep and forms to fill out, and cross-indexing. We never know when it might help in some way. Thanks again, and have a good night."

A good night indeed, she thought, as she closed and locked the door and turned the Security system back on. She took her bath, but it was not the leisurely, restful bath she had envisioned. Her head was too full of unanswered questions. She hurriedly put on her nightgown and robe, and tried to relax in her chair, but finally turned on the evening news after all. She had to do something. Why did the police want that information? He had told her nothing. Did they suspect that all was not above board with Miss Branish? She didn't even know if she was still living there--only that Betsy hadn't seen her for a while. How long? She didn't even know that. She told the police just what she had been led to believe, that Kendra, Betsy, and Miss Branish lived in the house. If Miss Branish was no longer there no one had informed her. She knew that her little granddaughter hadn't seen her. That was all.

She was only half watching and listening to the television when they announced that there had been another robbery even nearer their area and it had just happened. The man had been caught. Well, that was something to be thankful for anyway. He was where he belonged. There had also been another bomb scare at the new recreation building. The police had searched and found nothing, but had some leads on who might have sent in the alarm. Even though crime seemed to be much nearer home than it used to be, the police did seem to be doing a thorough job, and like Benny said, they are arresting a lot of the criminals. In spite of her security system, she still got up and checked both doors again. Her husband used to laugh at the way she had to check everything twice. If she balanced her checkbook with her calculator, she would go right over it again the old-fashioned way just to make sure the calculator was correct. If she had balanced it by hand the first time she would do it again with the calculator to check her own figures. She sat there a few minutes longer thinking of how wonderful life used to be when Kevin was still here. She went to bed but didn't sleep very well.

The next morning she was in the kitchen when the phone rang. It was Kendra. "Mother, how do you feel?"

"I'm fine--just got up and getting ready to make coffee. Why?"

"I'm coming over to pick up Betsy and take her to Andy's and...."

"Kendra, she's still asleep. Don't wake her up. Can't I keep her if you need to do something?"

"But you've already had her for so long and you must be tired, or have something else planned."

"We'll have a quiet day. I haven't anything in particular planned, so let her sleep. I want to know what's wrong though."

"Nothing is wrong. I just have a lot of things to do today and I can't take her with me."

"Kendra, something is wrong, and I wish you'd tell me what is going on. A policeman came here last night and wanted to know where you were and even asked where your tenant was. Of course I didn't know and I told him that you don't confide in me and...."

"I'm so sorry, Mom. He shouldn't have done that. Just continue to tell anyone who asks that you don't know. I want to tell you and I will as soon as I can. All right, if you're sure you feel up to it I'll leave Betsy with you and will call as soon as I can. Thanks, Mom. I love you--and stop worrying--please. Everything will work out fine."

What was it that Kendra knew and hadn't told her? Everything would work out fine? Then apparently it wasn't fine now. Something about her tenant? Did she suspect something was wrong too, and why did...?

Grammy," called Betsy sleepily, "can we read? Did you get the other cards to teach me?"

Millie turned to her granddaughter standing in the doorway in her pajamas rubbing her eyes, and had to laugh. "Let's get dressed and have some breakfast first, then we'll read." That's all her little granddaughter thought about these days, just learning to read.

After breakfast Betsy got out the name and picture cards and they started their make-believe school.

About an hour later Betsy exclaimed, "I hear Benny," as she jumped up and hurried to the door.

"Well hello, Betsy," called Benny. "Haven't seen you for a while, and you look quite a lot bigger to me."

"I'm supposed to be. I'm growing."

"Of course you are. What are you and your grandmother doing today?"

"She's teaching me to read and I can read the fronts of books."

"Did you know that your grandmother taught me to read too? Now I can read the fronts of books."

"You're big. I know you can read," she giggled.

"But I didn't learn until I was big, and you're learning now when you're little."

Millie came to collect her mail, and Betsy said, "Grammy, Benny said you teached him to read when he was already big."

"I guess I helped him a little," she said, than added, "It should be 'taught him to read'."

"I talked it wrong?"

Her grandmother hugged her and said, "No, you said it wrong," and the three of them were laughing.

"Your Grammy is a good teacher, Betsy, and if it hadn't been for her I wouldn't have this job now. And," turning to her grandmother he said, "I want to tell you that I helped Candy with her homework last night with the same example you gave me."

"What was that?"

"I asked you once if it was necessary to spend so much time on punctuation or 'squiggles and wiggles,' as Candy calls it. I told you I just wanted to learn to read, and you gave me the example about the dog named Rocky."

"Oh, I remember," and they both laughed.

"Well, got to run, but isn't this a great day?"

"It is now, Benny. As soon as we hear your whistle it's a great day."

"Good to see you girls," and he waved and went whistling on his way.

"He called us both girls, Grammy," giggled Betsy.

"And why don't we girls take a hot chocolate break from school?"

"Will you tell me the dog story, Grammy, the one you told Benny?"

"It wasn't a story. I was just showing him why it was important to use punctuation--that means commas, periods, question marks, things like that. We'll learn those later."

"But, not a story?"

"No, not a story, but I'll read you a story if you'd like."

After their hot chocolate Betsy and her grandmother played quiet board games, read their story, and later Millie tricked her into taking a nap. She had invented a game where they were supposed to pretend to be asleep, and it worked out just the way she had hoped, and they both got naps. By bedtime Kendra still hadn't called and her grandmother again helped Betsy get ready for bed, and she was soon sleeping soundly. Her grandmother relaxed in her comfortable wall hugger for a rest before getting ready for bed and the news.

The following week Betsy had again stayed overnight at her grandmother's house and was going to spend part of the next day there. Millie was in the kitchen making coffee the next morning when Kendra came in. "Oh," said her mother, startled, "I didn't hear the car."

"I didn't mean to frighten you. I was trying to be quiet in case you weren't up yet, and I parked on the street and didn't slam the car door. I just wanted to leave these coffee rolls for you. You mentioned getting some the other day and we forgot about it, so I went to the bakery on my way to work.

"Mommy," said Betsy, sleepily from the doorway, "do I have to go?"

"Not unless Grammy is tired of you," said her mother scooping her up in a hug.

Her grandmother said, "Then you don't have to go because Grammy isn't tired of you. We're going to have coffee rolls together and then have a fun day."

"And you have to have coffee with coffee rolls," said Betsy, looking sideways at her mother.

"Or milk, orange juice, or hot chocolate," said her grandmother, then to Kendra, "Have you got time to have something with us?"

Glancing at her watch, she said, "I don't think.... Oh sure, why not? I'll make time," and she got out the cups. "Run and get washed," she told Betsy, "and you can eat in your pajamas."

While they were eating they heard Benny's whistle. "Oh Boy, It's Benny," called Betsy, as she slid out of her chair and rushed for the door calling "I'll get the mail."

"Friend of all ages," laughed Kendra, as they heard the two of them visiting.

Her mother said, "Benny told me once that he learned to be cheerful by his grandfather's example. Once he told Benny that he couldn't hear out of his right eye and couldn't see out of his left ear. Benny had laughed and asked, "Do you know what you just said?" His grandfather told him, "Sure I do. If I had said it right you would have thought it was sad, but this way it made you laugh, didn't it?' Benny said he thought that was such a neat idea that he always tried to look on the bright side too. He also said his grandfather used the expressions 'fantabulous' and 'peachy keen' a lot, and when asked what those words meant, he told him they both meant 'pretty darned good'."

They both laughed, and Kendra said, "With an example like his grandfather no wonder he's always so cheerful."

"A smart grandfather," laughed Kendra, "and if you always tell the truth and always look on the bright side of everything, you can't miss."

While they were visiting Millie had also been trying to think of a way to get Andy into the conversation. She wanted to find out what both her tenant and Andy were up to, and what it was that Kendra was covering up from her. She couldn't seem to think of a way, and knew she had to find out some other way.

Betsy came in with the mail and put it on the table beside her grandmother, then climbed back into her chair. "Mommy, did you know that Grammy teached..." She looked at her grandmother questionably, who said "taught." Then Betsy continued, "taught Benny to read when he was big?"

"I think I did hear that," she said.

Her mother said to Kendra, "That seems to intrigue Betsy. He told me that he used one of my examples to help Candy with her homework. She was complaining about having to use all of those squiggles and wiggles around the words, it was supposed to read, "Rocky", yelled Kurt, "come here." Rocky happened to be a dog, and Kurt was his master. If there was no punctuation marks, it could as easily be read as, "Rocky yelled, "Kurt, come here." This would be rather strange for a dog.

I thought it was a good way to make someone remember the importance of good punctuation."

"It was, and to help Candy as well.

"You did have a story", said Betsy. "It was a story and you said it wasn't". She was looking puzzled at her grandmother.

"Then you tell me the story," said her mother.

"OK. Rocky said, `Come here, Kurt, and it was funny because Rocky was a dog."

"That's it?", asked her mother.

"That's it. It's a short story."

"Well, here's another short story," said her mother as she got up and hugged her daughter. "I've got to go to work. Bye Honey, Bye Mom," and she hurried out the door.

That afternoon when the phone rang, an excited Blanche said, "Have you turned on the TV this morning?"

"No. Why? What happened?"

"They have got the man and woman in custody who hi-jacked the car of that young college student. I'm so glad they are out of circulation. There may be others doing the same thing but at least those two are where they won't harm anyone else. They were arrested today in Plantville. A waitress who called the police recognized her. The grateful father of the student has promised the waitress an amount of $3,000. We need more people like her. Maybe I'll start driving again. Someone asked them if they had any leads on the survey scam and the police hinted that they have some good leads that they could not give out."

Both women felt better when they said their goodbyes. They hoped more arrests would follow and deter others from becoming criminals.

Millie sat in Kevin's recliner with a cup of coffee after the call and wondered about the policeman who had come to her door asking about the people living at Kendra's cottage. Did they suspect a link between Miss Branish and the scam--and possibly Andy too? She didn't know what Kendra knew, and if she suspected Miss Branish too. She also didn't know if Kendra was aware that Andy and her tenant even knew each other. She wondered what the something was that Kendra had said she'd tell her mother when she could. It must be something about Miss Branish. Now Millie wasn't so sure that Andy was involved, but it seemed strange that he had refused to go to Kendra's house. Even if Miss Branish and Andy did know each other, that didn't mean they were involved in anything illegal. When she got close to thinking of telling her daughter about her tenant and Andy knowing each other, she always got to the same point. She already knew that Kendra would not take her seriously, so why humiliate herself? She couldn't help but wonder where those two were and what was going on. Could she be Andy's mother and he was trying to protect her from something illegal? The police must suspect Miss Branish, or why try to find out where she was? And all Millie knew about anything was what information she could get from a four-year-old girl. Millie smiled as Betsy came into the room with a pile of books for their reading class.

CHAPTER 10

When Wednesday lunch day came, Millie went across to Kate's house and they decided to walk to the Waterfall Restaurant. As they started out, Kate asked Millie, "Did you see Benny this morning?"

"Benny? No. In fact I forgot to check to see if I had any mail. Why? Did you see him?"

"Well, I know you told us not to investigate her any more when you found out you were mistaken about Andy, but I still asked Benny if he delivered on Maison Street too, and when he told me he did, I asked him if he had ever seen Kendra's tenant. He said that once in a while he had a piece of mail for someone else at that address and had assumed Kendra had a visitor, but very soon after that he found the other mailbox and realized it was permanent. He said he had never seen the renter until a few mornings ago when a woman was coming out the door just as he arrived. He asked her if she was Miss Branish and she nodded. He told her he had some mail for her and she just pointed to her mailbox. She obviously didn't want to talk and hurried off. Now you know how friendly Benny is and even he couldn't charm her into saying a few words. Of course he said she was probably in a hurry and he shouldn't have spoken to her."

"Well I don't think Kendra has had more than a few words with her either. I think she is a pretty private person."

"Benny sure thinks a lot of you, Millie. He was telling me one day that he wouldn't be able to help Tyler with his homework if it hadn't been for you."

"Oh Pshaw, he would too. You know Benny--he'd have found a way to learn if I hadn't helped him. In fact, I'm sure Nancy would have helped him. She was an "A" student and taught school for two years before they were married."

"But he might not even have met Nancy if he hadn't been able to read," said Kate.

"Then I would be doubly thankful that he mentioned to me that he couldn't read well. They make a great couple and are doing a wonderful thing by adopting those children."

They took their time and it was an enjoyable walk, unlike the day they had walked to the subway entrance, and only about a third as far. They were fascinated with the beautiful mini waterfalls, which were on both sides of the entrance, and surrounded by foliage. They sat on the soft benches along the sides and stayed for a while admiring the restful scene before entering the dining room. The tables were attractively set with white tablecloths and flower arrangements on each, and assorted pastel napkins folded to petal shapes in each glass. These two patrons, however, asked to be seated on the screened-in porch with the bare wooden tables. From there they could see right into Longman's game room if the sun wasn't directly on it, but Millie was sure nothing would be solved by this maneuver. It was a nice day for a walk and lunch--and it would be considered just that.

The waitress asked them to sit on the bench by the entrance to the porch while she wiped off their table and the chairs around it. Then she proceeded to lay a white tablecloth and centerpiece like those on the inside tables.

When they were seated, Millie exclaimed, "How lovely. We didn't expect this service out here."

"We can't keep them set up out here because of the inevitable dust that seeps through the screening, but we do our best," said the waitress cheerfully. "All of our guests are important."

After the waitress had left them with their menus in front of them Kate remarked, "I had heard this was a really nice restaurant but had never been here. Now we'll find out if the food is as good as the atmosphere."

They both decided on the baked salmon special, and later agreed that it was exceptionally well cooked and nicely served. Suddenly Kate exclaimed, "Look, Millie, that woman--Kendra's tenant. See! Just looking at those kids, and I'll bet that look is a stare."

They watched for a moment in silence. Then Millie said, "How strange," as Miss Branish sauntered slowly back and forth, never turning her head away from the children. What in the world was she up to? They watched her for a while then looked away as they visited. After they had eaten they noted that she was still there, but soon Miss Branish slowly walked away, still looking back at the play area. They both watched her in silence as she suddenly started walking rapidly looking straight ahead and disappeared around the corner at the next street.

"What does it mean?" asked Millie. "Apparently she goes often if this is the third time that we know of her being there."

"It's not just that she's there, but she doesn't go inside where it seems as though she would be less conspicuous," said Kate. "It's obvious she's there just to watch the children and she stays so long. Maybe Belle was right when she said she might have lost a child at some time and just wants to watch them play--but why not go in and get something to eat or at least get a cup of coffee. I should think she could see them better from inside, and be more comfortable sitting down. That game room is mostly windows. Maybe she does have a little clearer view from outside, but there is a large area where the parents usually sit and the children are visible from inside too. That's what makes it seem like something ominous is going on. When I saw her before it looked as though she waved to someone inside, but it looks now as though she is hiding from those inside. Does that seem like something she would do?"

"You're asking me? Remember I haven't even met her," Millie told her. "The impression I have is that she could be capable of almost anything, but of course I don't know. I'm just confused at this point."

"You know I haven't met her either," said Kate, "but I've seen her and there is no question in my mind that the lady we just saw is Kendra's tenant and the one we followed. Let's come next Wednesday too. It's a nice walk if we take it slowly and the food is excellent and reasonable."

Millie was as sure as she could be that it was Kendra's tenant too. At least she thought that Miss Branish was probably back living at Kendra's now or she probably wouldn't have been in the area. "But why just Wednesdays?" she asked. "Let's see if she comes other days too. How about Friday next week?"

"I promised I would go into the library for a couple of hours on Friday," said Kate, but I should be back in plenty of time. They agreed on Friday if neither heard differently. They wanted days free for their granddaughters' visits. On their walk home Kate said, "Do you know, maybe she does just like children and she could even be a vegetarian and only goes where they serve the things she eats. We're probably being kind of silly about this."

"And maybe she isn't," said Millie, "and she's living in the house with my daughter and granddaughter."

"You're right, and it does seem strange."

That evening Millie started a notebook with notations of everything that she had found out so far about Miss Branish, and things she suspected. Kate was also keeping records since she was in the library a few hours for three mornings a week. There was always someone coming in bringing in bits of news. Millie and Kate would exchange notebooks to read at their next luncheon. Millie mentioned in her notations the possibility that Miss Branish could be connected with the Survey Scam. Kendra had said she had a very soft whispery voice. Millie knew the lady on the Survey also had that kind of a voice. She read all of her notations over again then thought to herself that it was only a smattering of information and although each item in itself didn't seem suspicious, when put together it added up to something questionable. Being in a hurry and not wanting to talk with anyone, not looking at people, sitting in restaurants in such a way that she wouldn't be noticed all added up to quite strange. Also seeming to keep from meeting Kendra, going out at night when no one would see her was another strange thing. The list went on and on, and together the items added up to at least, questionable actions. She was sure something was wrong and she hung onto the survey scam theory as the most likely, yet she had no proof of anything.

CHAPTER 11

Millie and Pauline were taking their walk around the block one afternoon when Millie was startled to see Miss Branish coming out of the Caledonian Baptist Church. Pauline was pointing out some flowers and didn't see the woman. While they were standing looking at the plantings in front of the building next door, Millie was busy wondering why the woman was in there at a time of no service. Then she thought it's just my overworked mind. She has a perfect right to go anywhere she wants, but there was certainly no service now. Suddenly she saw Andy and turned away so he wouldn't recognize her as he came down the steps of the church Miss Branish had left minutes before. She kept talking with Pauline as she turned her back to Andy, but couldn't help wondering. It was obvious that he didn't want to be seen with Miss Branish or he would have come out with her. What were they up to? And she was sure Kendra thought he was visiting some relatives. She was so upset wondering about it that Pauline asked if anything was wrong.

"No, no nothing is wrong. Why?"

"You just didn't seem to be with me all of a sudden."

"I'm sorry. I guess my mind did jump somewhere else for a few minutes. I was thinking about Kendra and wondering about that tenant of hers."

"I don't know her," said Pauline. "I've seen her and that day I asked her for the time she wasn't at all friendly. In fact she obviously didn't want to talk to me. I guess she isn't very sociable is she?"

"I don't think so. I've heard she just goes out for meals." They finished their walk with Millie trying to keep her mind on their conversation.

As soon as she got home she called Kate and told her what she had seen.

"Did Andy see you?" asked Kate.

"No, he went the opposite way and I turned so he couldn't see me if he looked back. I thought they were both away again and I wondered if Kendra knows he is back."

"It sure sounds like they are up to something. Do you know where Andy lives?"

"No, I don't. Just that he hasn't lived there long. And apparently he left in a hurry from the Hanover District. I keep telling myself that everyone seemed to think a lot of him in his home town, but then I wonder if he could have a secret side that they don't know about, and I wondered if Miss Branish is his mother and he is protecting her from something." "That's a thought. He could be," Kate said thoughtfully. "Maybe she has committed some crime and he hurried here to help her?"

"Well I was thinking along those lines," said Millie. "Some churches are always open and good places to meet."

"Be sure and put this all down in your note book," said Kate.

After Millie got through talking with Kate, she put the phone down, leaned back in her recliner and wondered what she should do. It seemed to Millie that Andy needed Kendra in this situation for some reason, and she didn't want her hurt. The last she had heard of Andy was when Kendra told her he had gone back to visit his family again after the summer play at the Rainbow School. Should she casually mention that she saw him come out of the Caledonian church? Why not? If he had misled Kendra about where he was going she should know it. And she wondered again what it was that her daughter was going to tell her when she could. Did she know something about her tenant and was now helping the police? Could that be it? Millie would not tell her daughter she had followed her tenant and saw her meet Andy, but it would surely be all right to tell her she saw someone who looked like her description of her tenant coming out of the Caledonian Church and after just minutes Andy had come out. Why not? That would let her know that they probably knew each other, wouldn't it? She would tell her the approximate time they were seen. They were quite likely the only ones in there as there was no church service near that time. Even if other people were in there they would have no trouble meeting for whatever business they had.

She picked up her notebook and wrote down everything, then got up and went out to the kitchen to see what she had to prepare for dinner.

Millie had forgotten about dinner and her mind was back on the renter. Was it possible that Miss Branish's first name was Catherine, and she was really a writer and not a criminal at all? She thought about it for a few minutes, and decided on a definite "No." Mable had called Millie to tell her she had seen a book named, "Calling Hours" written by Catherine "Branish" or "Branch". She couldn't seem to find it again and it was more likely that it had nothing to do with Miss Branish. Maybe she was a writer, but Millie was sure that something was not right. She counted off each thing again. Why did Andy move so quickly from his hometown to this area telling no one? Why did he immediately start seeing Kendra who owned the house the lady was in? How did he know this tenant who had only recently moved in? Why wouldn't he go to Kendra's house? Why were he and Miss Branish meeting away from where she lived? Then she wondered if she could tell Kendra that Andy came out of the church, but she didn't speak to him? Too far away? Of course that was it. She could tell Kendra she was too far away to speak to him. That should be enough so she would at least ask Andy if he knew her tenant. She would also know he wasn't home visiting his family.

The next time Kendra was there to bring Betsy, Millie did mention to her daughter about seeing Miss Branish, or someone who looked like her description of her tenant, coming out of the church. She told her daughter that a few minutes later Andy was coming out of the same door. She explained that she was too far away to speak without shouting, so just left. She wondered if they knew each other since they were in there at the same time.

Kendra had replied, "It could be," then asked, "Where were you and Pauline going? Just one of your walks?"

"Yes, but I was surprised as I thought you said Andy was visiting his family."

"Oh he came back a few days ago. And Mom, I'm really glad you're walking more. The doctor said you should, but to stop before you got too tired. You don't go too far, do you?"

"No, of course not." She was surprised that Kendra didn't seem to be interested at all in the fact that Miss Branish and Andy were in the church together. Or maybe she was interested and just wasn't showing her feelings. Well she had told her anyway. The way she said, "It could be" sounded as though she didn't care one way or the other.

After her mother had left, Betsy climbed into her grandmother's lap with her book. Millie asked her if she had seen Andy lately.

"No, and I miss Patty. Mom said we could go some day soon. It was kind of like having a sister and it was fun."

"I've noticed that you call your mother 'Mom' sometimes instead of 'Mommy'." She hugged her little granddaughter and said, "You're growing up too fast."

"Don't worry Grammy, Doctor Weaver said I'm just right for my age. When I was at camp, Michelle said we should start calling our mother 'Mom' now when we remember or people would think we are still babies."

"I can tell you're not a baby any more," said her grandmother. You're a good little girl, and your mother won't mind whether you call her 'Mom' or 'Mommy,' just like I don't care if your mother calls me 'Mom' or 'Mother'. Which one of these books do you want me to read?"

"The puppy one, then the bunny one," and Betsy handed her grandmother the puppy book.

Later while they were eating their lunch the phone rang and Millie went into the den to answer it. It was Mable, "I'm sorry if I got your hopes up," she told Millie, "but Marion just told me the book's author was Catherine Brandon. Miss Branish could still be an author, but this won't prove or disprove it. I can see why she was mistaken though. Brandon could look like Branish with a quick look. I'm really sorry and had hoped I could put your mind at ease. I shouldn't have called before I heard from her. I was just so excited and couldn't wait to know if Miss Branish's first name was Catherine."

"I did get my hopes up Mable, but only for a few minutes, then I realized that there were far too many things about Miss Branish that didn't quite click." Millie was thinking that If Miss Branish was mixed up in that survey scam or anything else; she hoped the police would uncover it soon, and she was really hoping Andy wasn't part of it. The police had said they had some good leads--and they had come asking about Miss Branish. She just hoped they would solve everything so Kendra would know the truth about her tenant as well as Andy. The longer it took, the more involved Kendra could become with Andy, and Millie was praying that Andy had as good a character as his towns people thought. She was still worried about the term "Lady's Man."

Then Mable brought her back to the present with, "So you still think she is up to something illegal?"

"I'm afraid I do, Mable. I tried to make allowances for her, but nothing can change facts, and there are too many things that don't add up right. Maybe I'm wrong, but... Anyway, thanks for calling. Right now I think I had better get back to my granddaughter. She is waiting patiently for me to read a book to her."

They both laughed, and Mable said, "I understand perfectly. I'll see you at our Bid Whist gathering on Thursday."

"Grammy," said Betsy, when her grandmother rejoined her at the table, "Will you wear this? I forgot to ask you when I got here," and she handed her the picture of a dog that she had colored. "I did it at school. Will you wear it all day?"

"I'd be honored to wear it. How do I keep it on?"

"Haven't you got a pin?"

"Yes, I believe I have." She got up and went to her sewing box to find a straight pin. "How's this?" she asked, as she pinned the dog to her blouse. "I'm being very careful," she said, "so I won't hurt him."

"It's OK, Grammy, it's just paper and it won't hurt him."

Her grandmother laughed, and hugged the little girl.

"I did it, Grammy, all by myself. Patty drawed one once and her father wore it all day."

Her grandmother refrained from correcting her this time and said, "Well, I'll wear it all day too. Thank you dear. Now let's finish our ice cream so we can read."

CHAPTER 12

Kate came over a little early on the day they had planned to go to the Waterfall Restaurant again so they could read each other's notebooks. Suddenly Kate said, "How about going to Longman's?"

"Instead of the Waterfall Restaurant?"

"I just happened to think if we go there today and if the lady happens to be there you can get a close-up of her, and we also might see someone inside who seemed to know she was out there. I'm pretty sure she waved to someone inside that time when I watched her leaving. It sure looked like it."

"It's all right with me. I think I'd rather ride today though--at least one way. I know your car is in the garage, but old faithful will be available. I'll call him."

"Of course. I thought you were limping a little, and I would prefer riding too."

Millie called "Handy Harry's Cab Service" to pick them up. When they went inside the restaurant Millie said, "I think I was in here a long time ago. Didn't they used to call this the School House?"

"Yes, they did. Originally they just catered to the kids. That was when they put in the game room, and it was so popular they added a lot of extra items to their menu and eventually had a chain of them. I guess that was when they changed the name to Longman's," added Kate. "I think there are four others in the state now."

They found a window seat for two and when the waitress came they both ordered the fried scallop roll, coffee, and a small green salad. Kate said thoughtfully, "They have delicious food here, but maybe this wasn't such a good idea as we can't see as well here as we could if we had gone to the Waterfall. See what a clear view we have of the Waterfall porch. Only if she happened to be out here when we came would it have helped us. I haven't seen anyone in here who seems to be looking outside either. Have you?"

"I have noticed that most people are visiting with others and not even looking around," said Millie, "but others are coming in, so I'll keep watching as new ones enter."

When they had finished their lunch and were sipping their coffee Kate suggested that she go outside as though she was looking for something she might have dropped. If the woman happened to be there she would come back and tell Millie, then they would go out together.

The woman hadn't come and Kate felt silly for suggesting they come to Longman's as she turned back toward the restaurant. While she was gone Millie had been watching those people entering. Occasionally she would look around to see if Miss Branish might possibly be in the restaurant, or maybe notice someone in there who seemed to be looking out.

When Kate came back inside, people were standing around Millie who was bent across the little table.

"What happened? What's wrong?" She rushed to Millie, who had no color in her face.

"We called 911 and help is on the way," said the manager. A man who was feeling her pulse called out, "She's got a pulse, thank God." The ambulance soon arrived and the medics rushed into the restaurant with a gurney, and Millie was soon on the way to the hospital and Kate was with her.

"What happened, Millie," she asked. Millie didn't open her eyes or answer her.

The medic on the opposite side of Millie put down his stethoscope and said, "The man who called said she just fell across the table, and couldn't seem to talk, and she was very pale. They found a pulse after they called us, but she hasn't opened her eyes or spoken."

"Millie, talk to me," said Kate over and over. She was holding her hand and finally Millie opened her eyes and looking bewildered asked, "Where are we going in this noisy thing?"

"We're taking you to the hospital," she said in relief.

"Oh no," she said weakly, "I want to go home. I'm all right."

The medic explained to her what she had done and why she had to have a check-up. Then no doubt she would be able to go home, and then he asked Kate, "Are you a relative?"

"Just a friend--a good friend."

"Can you call her family?"

"No," shouted Millie, as she tried to sit up.

They were at the hospital and soon had her in the Emergency Room. After a thorough check-up they had contacted her doctor Who was given the data and, after some questions, he gave his permission for her to go home. Kate had not called Kendra, as Millie had not wanted her to, and she was thinking she might be able to talk her into calling her daughter herself once they got home.

When they arrived home and were seated in Millie's living room she asked, "All right, Millie, what happened?"

"I got dizzy and the next thing I knew we were wailing our way to the hospital, but don't tell Kendra. I'm all right, so why worry her?"

"Has this ever happened before?"

"No, never, and I'm sure it won't happen again, and apparently I just fainted."

"But it could happen again if you don't even know what caused it."

"I do know what caused it, she said slowly, I was looking around the restaurant and saw some kids going to that game room. I turned to look at them and saw colored bubbles. A woman in there was running a bubble machine for a little girl and I...I.... Kate, Betsy told me that one time when Andy and her mother took them to lunch that she and her friend Patty played in a room afterwards where a lady let them make colored bubbles from a machine. I don't know where they were, but all I could think of was that Kendra's tenant might have been watching them. It must have been a Longman's Restaurant."

"So that's it. Even if she happened to be watching them she couldn't get to them. Really, there's nothing to worry about. It's strange but not anything to worry about."

"No? Then why did you think it was important enough to tell me about the woman staring at the children?"

"I'm not sure. It seems kind of silly now. And even if you were startled by what you saw and thought, why would you pass out? That's not normal, and I think you should tell Kendra about it. Do you feel all right now?"

"Absolutely. I'm fine, and if I ever have a feeling anything like that I promise I'll tell her. It was just a flash of terrible fright. That would not happen again, I'm sure."

Kate stayed with her for quite a while. Then, satisfied that she was indeed all right, she left for home. She sat in the recliner for a long time just thinking. Where had Betsy and Patty been playing where there were colored bubbles? Could that woman have been watching when they were playing? She didn't even know which Longman's they had been in, or when they had been there, but she was frightened. Not knowing was worse than knowing. She hadn't given it much thought until today when she suddenly wondered about those colored bubbles and what this staring at the kids was all about--and if the woman was there at the time Betsy and Patty were. If she was there, was she staring at Betsy? Which one of them was she staring at, and why? Did she have a camera? Could she have been taking pictures? Another possibility was that other game rooms or play areas might have colored bubble machines too. It might not have been at any Longman's. It could have been at a park, couldn't it? No, it seemed as though Betsy had mentioned eating first. Could other restaurants have one of those machines? They probably could. If they were made, then other restaurants could buy them too. She didn't know of any others that even had game rooms, but there could be. Of course there could probably be a bubble machine without having a game room. She wasn't sure what Betsy had told her anyway. She decided she wasn't going to worry about it any more. As Kate had said, no harm could be done by being stared at, and she was right and this was silly. It meant nothing. She would put it out of her mind.

The next day Kendra brought Betsy to her mother and was coming to pick her up in about two hours. Millie made sure she didn't look tired and moved around a little faster than usual so Kendra would know she was just fine. After she left, Betsy ran to get the cards with the words and pictures so she could learn to read. Before they started, her grandmother said, "Do you remember you told me one time a lady let you and Patty play with a bubble machine that made colored bubbles?"

"Um, it was fun. I never saw such lots of colored bubbles. Will you take me sometime Grammy?"

"I don't know where you were, dear. Was it a long ways off?"

"Yup a real long ways and we could look out like a big window all around. Can we read?"

"Hop up in my lap and we'll read."

As she sat in her grandmother's lap she started holding up each card and reading the word. Millie thought, this may be the way they are teaching now with these pictures and one word under each, but it's not the right way. I'm going to teach her phonetics. After a few more cards she said to Betsy, "I think that's enough of the pictures, let's learn the way the older children learn--without pictures.

"I'm big now?"

"No, not big, but big enough so you can learn to read another way."

CHAPTER 13

One evening a few weeks later Millie was dozing in the recliner when she was startled awake by the phone. It was Kendra. "Are you going to be up for a while, because if you are, we want to come over for a short visit."?

"Betsy is asleep," her mother said.

"I was sure she would be. I couldn't call any sooner anyway. Stay up, Mother, but close Betsy's door. I don't want her to wake up. We'll be right over. We have news--Great news," and she hung up.

Millie automatically hurried over and closed the door to Betsy's room. It had to be Andy who was with Kendra and what could the great news be? Were they getting married? She gasped, and her hand flew to her head. Oh no, what if that was it? She knew she should have told her daughter all she knew regardless of how she knew it. She had been ready for bed and dozing in the recliner. Now she hurriedly got dressed again and straightened up the living room a little. Oh dear, why hadn't she told her? But she had told her that her tenant and Andy were in the church together and she hadn't seemed interested. She might have thought it was just a coincidence. What if they got married and Kendra was walking into some kind of a trap? Someone had called Andy a "Lady's Man". Did that mean that all the ladies liked him, or that he liked too many ladies? What was meant by the phrase "a lady's man"? He hadn't been around very much of late. Could he have other women that he was seeing as well, and was Kendra just a cover-up for something else? Oh dear, it wasn't too late. They weren't married yet--were they? Could that be the news? Could they have gotten married already? Maybe she wouldn't have time to talk with Kendra alone. If she was too late, she'd never forgive herself for not telling her immediately what she knew.

When they arrived it was indeed Andy with Kendra, and there was also an older man with them whom Andy introduced as his father, Albert Calendar. His father seemed very pleasant and he told Millie he had been wanting to meet Kendra's mother. She was thinking, "Oh dear they must be getting married and he wanted to meet his son's future mother-in-law. She was hoping she would have time to talk with Kendra before that could happen."

Andy then jumped to say, "It's a long story, and unbelievable by those who knew him, but my father was accused of committing a robbery. Although completely innocent, several people swore he was the man they had seen coming out of the Spencer National Bank, and he was arrested. He didn't think he had any chance to clear himself with their word against his and no way to prove that he had just happened to be out walking in that area. Because of the lax security and his desperation, he managed to slip away, get across two streets, down to the subway stairs and board a subway car that was just leaving. He got to a friend, who knew him well enough to know he could never have robbed a bank, and he was able to help him." Andy suddenly shouted, "'Yippee, Dad. You're free!' Oh that felt good, he added. It has been so long," then turning to Millie he said excitedly, "I'm sorry Mrs. Houston, but I think it just hit me that he is no longer a hunted man. If you only knew my father you would understand how unthinkable that was to me."

Millie had been wondering why Andy was telling her this information about his father being accused of a crime while his father was right there. Now she understood that he was innocent.

"Mother," Kendra said, interrupting Andy, "sit down right here. Now remember I told you I would explain everything soon? Well, you know how anxious you have been to meet my tenant, Miss Branish? Mother, this is Miss Branish," as she pointed to Andy's father.

Millie gasped then asked in bewilderment, "Oh, oh my! My goodness!" They couldn't help laughing at her confusion.

When they got serious again, Andy quickly continued his explanation to Mrs. Houston. "The friend who helped my father supplied him with a woman's clothing, a wig and all."

Andy's father then said to her, "Mrs. Houston, Of course I knew I was harmless and wouldn't harm your daughter--but I wouldn't have rented the room if I had known a little girl lived there too. When I found it out, I simply stayed out of sight as much as possible. Neither would I have rented so near the police station if I had known they were there." Then he laughed, and said, "Maybe it was just as well I didn't know, as they probably wouldn't be looking for me that near them. At least it wouldn't be the first place they would look. A dear friend of a friend, Mrs. Richards, spoke to a teacher neighbor of hers and they found me the little room in Kendra's house.

"My son, Andy, got a job teaching nearer to me so I could occasionally see my little granddaughter, Patty. All I could think of when I was arrested was that she shouldn't see her grandfather in prison or his picture in the papers. I could only see her when she was asleep or she would surely have mentioned a lady coming to see her--and might even have recognized something about me. Then we thought of a way to see her when she was awake. Several times we arranged things so I could see her at a Longman's Restaurant where I could watch her playing and having fun undetected, but I just had to see her. I was scared meeting Andy and going to see Patty, but it was a chance I decided to take. We were very careful and it worked. My son's housekeeper took Patty to Longman's and let her go into the game room. If I had been caught and arrested I would have some memories and pictures of her. Anyway, it's over now. The real robber was caught tonight and I don't wonder that people thought I was he. I hate to think I look so much like a common thief. I knew I was renting under false pretenses but I couldn't go to anyone who knew me and trusted me, as the authorities would be checking everyone who had ever had any contact with me. Mrs. Richards was going to rent to me, but we decided it would be too dangerous as she is a close friend of one of my cousins. It was such a relief when Andy told me that he had confided in Kendra and she wanted to help. I couldn't very well contact a lawyer, so Kendra and Andy took over that part for me. Kendra knew a lawyer whom she was positive could be discreet. They met him in different places on my behalf and were putting together all of the facts when my look-alike decided to rob another bank. Thank God, he did, or I might never have been able to go free. That just shows how easy it can be for an innocent person to end up in jail, or at least go through hell before being proven innocent."

"I won't pretend that this wasn't a big shocker," Kendra laughed. "It was staggering, but I was sure Andy wouldn't make up something like that and I agreed to just keep pretending I didn't know anything, but help out in any way I could."

Millie Houston had been sitting as though in shock, but was thinking that if she had called the police with an anonymous tip to check out Miss Branish, what a mess she would have made of that innocent man's life and his loved ones too. She said, "Sit down everyone. I think...I guess...maybe some coffee...?" She started to rise.

Kendra put her hand on her mother's shoulder and said, "Stay right there, Mother," as each found a seat, then she headed for the kitchen. "I'll put the coffee on, and find something. We do need to celebrate. What a relief!"

As Kendra left the room Andy said, "I want you to know, Mrs. Houston, that when I met Kendra I had no idea in the world that her house was where my father was renting. I was flabbergasted when I found it out and didn't dare go there as I was sure detectives would find out I was his son, even though I was still using my stage name. What would the chances be of my meeting the very woman who owned the house where my father was hiding? Anyway, we got away with it. After I had been seeing Kendra for a few weeks I realized I could trust her--so told her everything. It didn't take long before I knew her well enough to make that decision. I'm sure she wondered at all of my excuses to meet her at different places instead of coming to her house. I knew shortly after meeting her that I wanted to keep seeing her. It was sure a relief when I could tell her the truth. And the strange thing was that she had decided just about at that same time that she could trust me and ask my advice about her tenant. We were both relieved when we decided to trust each other. All of the secrets we had been keeping weren't comfortable for either of us. And believe me, it was an enormous relief when we heard the news tonight that my father was cleared."

Millie was thinking that the secrets she had been keeping were not comfortable either.

Mr. Calendar said, "If that guy hadn't decided to rob another bank and hadn't got caught this time--Gosh, I don't know what would have happened. The authorities were getting too close. We were in the process of finding another place for me to move to. It was only a matter of time before they would have found me. They were going to every house in the area. Andy and Kendra helped me and thank God our luck held out long enough for them to catch and arrest the robber. I suppose this was the last section they searched, as it was so near the police station. I'm sorry they bothered you Mrs. Houston."

"Now that I know, I understand," she told him. "You are innocent, and everyone will know it now. I know it's a minor thing but I'm curious. How did you happen to choose the name Branish?"

"I was thinking that I would have to vanish and from that I hopped from 'Vanish'-'Banish'-'Branish' and decided 'Branish' would be a good name. I doubt if anyone actually has that name."

Millie was glad she hadn't gone any farther in her search of the name 'Branish', especially with Joey Branish still in prison.

Andy said, "When my father found out that Kendra knew everything and wanted to help, he told me to have her act in front of everyone as though she had no idea that he was anyone but Miss Branish, the writer."

"Are you really a writer?" asked Millie.

"Gosh, no," and he laughed.

Andy said, "When Dad told me he was masquerading as a woman writer I was really scared. I knew there was no way he could talk like a woman, and he had never typed in his life. Turning to his father he asked, "I never thought to ask you when I was with you, but why in the world did you pick writing as your career?"

"It was all I could think of that would keep me inside most of the time. Just about everything else I'd have had to go out to work every day, and where could I have spent my days until time to come home from work? And writers usually keep to themselves when on a project. It just seemed to be the answer." Andy was nodding his head. "That does make sense. Not many choices, were there? Kendra said you arrived with a typewriter, or I think she called it a word processor, a suitcase, and a laundry bag. You must have done some typing up there."

"I actually did tap tap at the keys at first in case anyone could hear me, and I got so I could type (or make the sound of typing) pretty fast with one finger of each hand. It worked best when I used the same two fingers and keys over and over. The reason you didn't ask me before was because you were too busy telling me what I was doing wrong in trying to act like a woman." Both men started laughing.

Kendra returned to the living room with a tray of coffee, cups, fixings, cookies, coffee cake, and sharp cheddar cheese, and set it on the side table. She said, "Help yourselves everyone." Mr. Calendar served Millie her refreshments. After he had got his own serving he picked up his coffee and took a big swallow. "I don't have to sip any more. It helped trying to think of these things. I would have gone crazy if I had just thought about the accusations against me and whether they would find me."

Millie said, "A friend of mine saw you coming out of a church one day and asked you for the time. She said you didn't answer her and acted as though you didn't want to be seen."

"How did your friend know who I was?" he asked in bewilderment.

"Apparently you had eaten in her son's restaurant a few times and he lives across the street from Kendra's house."

"Wow, I guess I'm luckier than I had realized. I wonder why she was interested enough to even mention that incident."

Millie wasn't about to tell him that she had been questioning her friends about her daughter's strange secretive tenant, and replied, "A lot of the people in this area have lived here a long time, even went all through school together, so we just plain gossip, and that happened to come up when someone asked how Kendra was doing." Then she added, "Betsy told me she didn't see you at all except when you went out at night."

Mr. Calendar replied, "I don't think little Betsy even knew I was still there after a while. Her mother found her looking out the window one night and Betsy told her she watched the lights and sometimes saw the lady up stairs go out. Kendra told Andy and he told me. From then on I simply took a different route so Betsy wouldn't see me any more--but I was right there."

Andy told her, "When that man robbed another bank and was caught, the police thought he was the one they had arrested for the last robbery also, and had escaped. The robber had gone free and it was my dad they had been hunting for. That guy must have been really bewildered when they questioned him about how he had got away and where he had been hiding. As soon as he was caught and we saw the picture of him in the paper, my father knew they would have it straightened out soon. We had no way of knowing at first that this robber was the same one who had robbed the Spencer National Bank, or that he looked so much like my father. I suppose they didn't want to advertise, unless they had to, that they had been lax enough for one of their prisoners to escape. We knew they were diligently hunting for my father. We were all hugging and dancing when that guy was caught!" Andy put his arm around Kendra and added, "And now that it's over, Kendra and I can go anywhere we want without looking over our shoulders, and with no worries about our families."

Kendra said, "But I think the authorities owe your dad a public apology--and more."

His father replied, "Thanks, Kendra, but tonight's news should tell the public. It satisfies me anyway. And I hold no animosity toward the people who identified me as the robber. None of them knew me, and I certainly do resemble him. Can you imagine how it felt to see several people pointing at me and saying, "He did it." "That's the man," and "I saw him clearly"? I didn't even know at first what I was supposed to have done. One officer had hold of my arm while they were questioning the witnesses, but they hadn't cuffed me. I probably didn't look like the type who would try to escape or they wouldn't have been so careless. Believe me I was desperate, and desperation can change people. I was on the Track Team in college, maybe a little rusty but I can still move. I just took a flying leap away from that officer and was off running. I'm sure they were embarrassed about it, as I'm obviously much older than those young fellows and there wasn't much publicity at first. I made it to Perry Richard's store. I stayed in the back of his store until he found the clothes, wig, and the other props I needed. Then he and Mrs. Richard arranged for me to go to Kendra's to see the room I was hoping to rent. Perry and I have been friends for years and we both knew I wasn't safe there." Then turning to her mother, "I'm just sorry you were worried about your daughter and granddaughter, Mrs. Houston. I must have seemed awfully secretive to you."

She hesitated, and then said with a twinkle in her eye, "I'm glad I finally met you, Miss Branish." Everyone laughed. Then Millie asked him, "How did you manage to talk like a woman?"

"That was really the hardest part of all and the reason I had to stay away from everyone. I thought of the movie, 'Mrs. Doubtfire' but couldn't seem to remember how her, I mean his, voice sounded. I tried to make my voice higher but didn't sound anything like a woman until I tried kind of half talking and half whispering, but it was a strain. The worst time of all was when I first went to your daughter's house to see about renting the room, as I had to talk so much answering all of her questions. I was really sweating. The sun was bright in her living room and I kept wondering if I had shaved close enough. After that interview was over and she had agreed to rent me the room I was greatly relieved. I tried not to see too much of her, or anyone else for that matter, so I wouldn't have to talk. My throat was sore for a couple of weeks after that interview. It was hard ordering in a restaurant too. I got so I would just say a few words and point to what I wanted on the menu. After a while of this I thought of whispering 'laryngitis' then pointing to the menu. I was very nervous eating in restaurants. I looked at a waitress' hands one day as she served me, then at my big hands, and that seemed like a sure give-away, but there was no way I could hide them and eat. Occasionally I got something 'to go' and tucked it in a large bag that I carried and went back to my room to eat it, but I still had to use my hands to pay the bill. I bought snack foods, of course, and bread, peanut butter, that sort of thing and snacked in my room some.

Millie said, "Kendra told me that you liked eating out as you didn't like to cook."

"This set-up had to work as there was no way to cook. I had to tell her I liked eating out. Anyway, it all came together. I had to get out of that little room or go crazy cooped up there. When Kendra and Betsy were camping I couldn't go out, as I wanted the neighbors to think I was gone too. I used blackout curtains and because Kendra gave me permission to use her kitchen and move around the house, it all worked out."

Andy turned to Millie and said, "I knew you didn't approve of me, Mrs. Houston, as a companion to your daughter, but couldn't think of any way I could reassure you and not let everything out in the open. I guess it was a rough time for all of us."

To cover up her embarrassment, Millie said, "It wasn't that I didn't approve of you Andy--just that I didn't think Kendra had known you very long. I guess I was just being a mother." Suddenly she thought of something, and laughed and said, "I heard you had to wear a dog all one day for your daughter."

"Yes, I did, Betsy must have told you. I pinned it to my tie and wore it all day."

"Well, I wore one all day too," she said. As they were all laughing, Millie was thinking she was glad the mystery of the blue tie was solved. No wonder Andy and Miss...his father were laughing about it. She would have to remember that there never was any Miss Branish.

They were all so relieved and happy that they were really in a celebrating mood. It was the end of a difficult time for all of them, but in so many different ways. Andy and his father left very soon. Andy had grabbed Kendra and whirled with her a few times in exuberance telling Kendra that he'd see her tomorrow, and to be thinking about how she wanted to celebrate the next night.

After they were gone, her mother told Kendra how sorry she was that she didn't just let her handle her own life. "I was so worried about you but I shouldn't have tried to get involved. I know now that I only made things a lot more difficult for you, and I'm so sorry. Are you and Andy planning marriage?" she asked her.

"No, Mother. Maybe someday--who knows? Right now we are just happy to be able to go anywhere we want and know that our families are safe. Now we can really concentrate on getting to know each other. His wife died of cancer when Patty was only two, so we do have a lot in common and comfort each other."

"Kendra," said her mother, "when I went over to your house to get that list for you, weren't you concerned that it would frighten Andy's father to hear someone come into the house?"

"No, Andy and I were in touch all of the time and he had told his father you would be over and just to be quiet, so he was listening for you. I couldn't very well have either Andy or his father send me the list either."

"I had so many thoughts running around in my head," said her mother, "and none of them were right." Benny happened to mention to me that he had seen you one evening getting into a car with two men. I worried a lot about that and wondered who they were and...."

"Oh Mom, I'm sorry you were worried. That was probably an attorney friend of Andy and mine. We met him often and he was doing a great job in gathering material to defend Andy's dad."

"I should have known you could handle anything that came up," said her mother. "I don't know why I thought I could do it better. Never again. Promise!"

They had a lovely visit, both so happy that their problems were over, and Kendra left a message for Betsy that she would be over in the morning to have breakfast with her and Grammy, then take her home.

After Kendra had left, Millie called Belle; the only one of her Bid Whist friends whom she knew would still be up. She told her the best she could of the what had happened, and asked her to notify Kate and Mable in the morning and she would talk with them later.

"I guess it was a good thing that I gave up my thoughts of a detective's career, and taught piano instead," and they both were laughing as they agreed.

After talking with Belle, Millie sat in Kevin's chair and vowed to herself that there would be no more meddling in Kendra's affairs. She really had let her imagination run amok. Obviously strange things happen in real life--but stranger ones in your mind.

AFTERMATH

Eventually Millie did pay off that awful debt for the security system and her life was really back to normal--but falling for that scam would remain her little secret, as well as the reason for selling her piano. She was again walking slowly around the block with Pauline nearly every morning and meeting often with her Bid Whist friends.

The instigators of the survey scam were caught and that little project was shut down when the ringleaders were arrested. Best of all she was no longer frightened of the evening news, or anything else-- and she slept well. What a difference that security system had made! So it wasn't all a loss. She had simply traded her piano for peace of mind.

Kendra had rented out the little room to another teacher who worked with her and it turned out to be comfortable for everyone. Eventually the teacher got married and left, and Kendra was making enough salary by then so it wasn't necessary to rent it again. She and Andy were almost always together now and were talking marriage.

Millie had to admit that Kendra did indeed know how to live her own life without any help from her mother, and she thoroughly approved of her daughter's choice of company.

One day several months later Millie received a letter from someone she had never heard of. Who in the world was Nancy Morrison? She opened it to read:

Dear Mrs. Houston,

About a year and a half ago I called you to help in a survey. You were expecting company but were kind enough to give me a few minutes of your time. It was about appliances. I'm sure you have forgotten, but I never will. My husband had died the year before, and I was trying hard to take care of our little girl. I thought the Consumer Products job would be perfect as I could do it from home, but so many people were rude to me and even hung up on me that I was ready to give up. I decided one more call would tell me whether I should keep at it or quit. You were my next call, and so nice that I just knew it was a sign to hang in there.

With the confidence I got from talking with you I kept trying. Finally another nice woman told me about a permanent job. I am now working at a child-care organization where I can take Margie with me and it's working out beautifully. I have just recently found my records with your name and address so I could write to thank you. I'm sorry it has taken so long. You'll always be in our prayers.

Nancy and Margie Morrison

Millie stared at that letter in stunned stupor for several minutes, and then in her mind she relived that whole horrible experience--those awful nights in the closet, the sleepless and frightening nights that followed, and her lovely piano that she sorely missed. Then she breathed a long sigh and read the letter again. When she came out of the shock and started thinking clearly again, her first reaction was relief. This one hadn't been a scam at all. There had been no reason for that awful fright and the problems connected with it including the loss of her piano.

She didn't know whether to laugh or cry. Finally a chuckle started deep within her, then gradually turned into a real laugh. She was thinking, I was wrong about this being a scam and I was wrong about Miss Branish and Andy being some kind of shady characters. In fact I was wrong about everything. As I told Belle, it was a good idea that I learned to play the piano. I even gave some thought to Kendra's suggestion of trying my hand at writing suspense stories, but I have decided I'll give my imagination a rest and let others do the detecting and writing the books while I continue my favorite hobby of reading. And as she settled in her recliner she started thinking about Kendra's and Andy's wedding. She knew Kendra loved yellow roses, so there should surely be yellow and white roses and.... Then she shut her mind off. No, she would not even think about it, and if they wanted her help they would surely ask. She picked up her book and leaned back to read with a smile on her face.

####

Printed in the United States
By Bookmasters